DOROTHY CANFIELD FISHER

D1084162

-84

A Formal Feeling

ALSO BY ZIBBY ONEAL

The Language of Goldfish

A FORMAL FEELING

a novel by Zibby Oneal

The Viking Press
New York

With special thanks to Zibby Alexander

First edition
Copyright © 1982 by Zibby Oneal
All rights reserved
First published in 1982 by The Viking Press
625 Madison Avenue, New York, New York 10022
Published simultaneously in Canada by Penguin Books Canada Limited
Printed in U.S.A.   1 2 3 4 5 86 85 84 83 82

Grateful acknowledgment is made to Little, Brown and Company
for permission to reprint Poem #341, "After Great Pain,"
from *The Complete Poems of Emily Dickinson*, edited by
Thomas H. Johnson. Copyright 1929 by Martha Dickinson Bianchi;
© renewed 1957 by Mary L. Hampson.

Library of Congress Cataloging in Publication Data
Oneal, Zibby.   A formal feeling.
Summary: Sixteen-year-old Anne, home from boarding school for the
holidays, has difficulty accepting her new stepmother's presence
in the house that holds so many memories of her dead mother.
[1. Death—Fiction.   2. Stepmothers—Fiction]   I. Title.
PZ7.0552Fo   [Fic]   82–2018   ISBN 0–670–32488–4   AACR2

TO BOB

After great pain, a formal feeling comes—
The Nerves sit ceremonious, like Tombs—
The stiff Heart questions was it He, that bore,
And Yesterday, or Centuries before?

The Feet, mechanical, go round—
A Wooden way
Of Ground, or Air, or Ought—
Regardless grown,
A Quartz contentment, like a stone—

This is the Hour of Lead—
Remembered, if outlived,
As Freezing persons, recollect the Snow—
First—Chill—then Stupor—then the letting go—

—EMILY DICKINSON

One

The plane circled the airport twice, banking above the dark clouds like a gull over water, and then began its descent. Anne closed her eyes and felt the smooth dropping begin. When she looked again, the terminal was just below and the red lights on the landing strip winked beneath them.

The wheels bumped ground. The engines roared. Anne let out her breath. She distrusted landings.

The man in the seat beside her began putting papers into his briefcase. "Looks like they've had some snow," he said, nodding toward the runway beyond the window. The wet pavement shone like glass, reflecting lights already burning in the terminal, although it was only two-thirty in the afternoon.

Anne pulled her small bag from under the seat. The man handed down her coat from the overhead bin and said, "I hope it's a good vacation." Anne thanked him.

She hadn't thought of the vacation in terms of good or bad. Coming home from school for Christmas was simply what everyone did. Last night, up and down the corridor, the girls, packing and chatting, had stirred the air with their excitement. Anne's roommate threw armloads of clothes into the suitcase on the bed. "No more school for three weeks, Cameron!" she'd said to Anne with a jubilation Anne couldn't share. It didn't really matter whether she was at home or at boarding school. Maybe, on balance, she would have preferred school.

When the line of passengers began to move, she followed the man with his briefcase down the aisle and out into the chute that led to the terminal. Her bag bumped against her leg as she walked, neither slowly nor quickly, toward the waiting room.

Spencer was cutting class to meet her plane. He had said he didn't mind. As she emerged into the brightly lighted terminal, she looked for him in the crowd waiting at the gate. She saw him almost at once, tall and thin at the back of the crowd, wearing his old green parka, blinking near-sightedly at the stream of people coming off the plane. She waved.

Spencer began sidling his way toward her, smiling ironically as she remembered he'd taken to doing in his freshman year. "So there you are." He said it as though he had run into her on the street, she thought, and not as if she had been away for three months.

"Here I am," she replied. "Do you want to carry my bag?"

She glanced sideways at her brother and was somehow reassured by the sameness of him. If he had kissed her or said the sort of thing most people say to arriving travelers, it would have bothered her. Instead, he said, "Did you check your other stuff?"

"This is all I brought."

"For three *weeks*?"

"I don't need much. There are a few things still at home."

Carols blared over loudspeakers in the terminal. The newstands were bright with tinsel and plastic holly. "I found a parking place almost outside the door," Spencer said. "The reward for virtuous living, I guess."

The glass doors to the street slid open for them, and they walked the short distance to the car. "Has it been snowing?"

"More like rain," Spencer said. "I'm dreaming of a wet Christmas—isn't that how the song goes?"

Anne tugged at the car door and climbed into the front seat. "Thanks for cutting your class," she said. "I hope it doesn't matter."

"It's the one I usually sleep through anyway." Spencer started the car and put it into reverse. The gears ground and shuddered. "Same old car," he said.

"You don't put the clutch in far enough," Anne said automatically.

"You sound like Mother."

Spencer tried the gearshift again, and this time it slid

into reverse. "Dad was sorry he couldn't meet you. He lectures at two, and then he has a seminar."

"I know." It was all right that her father couldn't come. She needed this return to be gradual.

Spencer eased the car out into the traffic. "He—they'll—be home about six."

Anne looked out the window at the dirty gray day and then at Spencer's profile. "How is it at home?" she asked carefully.

"Fine. I'm not there much. But I've been going home Sundays for supper, and it's fine."

Anne turned toward the window again. "I can't imagine it."

Spencer pulled into the lane of cars heading away from Detroit. He flicked on the radio. Instantly there was a blast of music. "So how's school?" he asked, turning down the volume.

Anne shrugged. "All right. Classes, you know. Eating. Studying. I've been running cross-country this fall."

"Yeah?" Spencer said. "Do you like it?"

"Running?"

"All of it."

"I guess." She really couldn't say. When she thought about it, she could smell the waxed corridors between classrooms, the odor of crushed grass on the hockey field, the smell of shampoo in the showers—but that had nothing to do with liking it or not.

"The work's hard."

"Still? Even after a year?"

"That's the point, isn't it? 'A rigorous educational curriculum' is what they advertise."

Spencer grunted.

"I can manage," she said.

The expressway stretched ahead of them, wet and absolutely straight. Like a Roman road, her mother always said, utterly uncompromising. Spencer drifted into the passing lane and back. For a while they drove in silence. Anne listened to the swipe of the wipers and the jingle of a muffler commercial coming low over the radio. "Do you wish you hadn't gone back?" Spencer said.

"Oh, no." Anne turned to look at him. "Oh, no, I wouldn't want to be home now."

Ahead was their exit and beyond it the drive-in theater that, so far as Anne could remember, had always been closed. Spencer turned onto the exit ramp, and the cars on the expressway swept on behind them. Anne could see the University's bell tower in the distance, solid gray against the gray horizon. Just to the left of it, a block away, her father would be finishing his lecture. She could picture him, hunching slightly, glancing at his watch, trying to hurry through two more things he wanted to say. And then, as abruptly as the image had come to her, she put it away.

They drove the few miles to town, listening to the three o'clock news. At the edge of the campus Spencer stopped to let a crowd of students pour across the street ahead of the car. "Everyone looks frantic at this time of year," he said.

"When is the semester over?"

"The twenty-second. Next week is finals."

There were only a few blocks remaining now. The house on Lincoln Street was close to the campus. She saw it at the end of the block as soon as Spencer turned the corner—the big white frame house with the magnolia tree in front. The tree was bare now, of course, but in spring it was laden with heavy mauve blossoms. Beneath it, years before, her mother had planted a bed of blue hyacinths.

All at once it seemed to Anne that things were moving too fast. She turned toward her brother. "Go around the block once, Spencer."

He glanced at her. Then he nodded. "All right."

They came in the side door, up the steps to the kitchen. It was the way they always came in.

On the kitchen table was a scatter of mail—torn envelopes, bills, a schedule of concerts. In the sink were two dirty coffee cups and the soggy remains of breakfast toast. Anne stood looking around her. Spencer hoisted her bag onto the kitchen stool.

"Do you want me to take this upstairs?" he said. "I'll carry it up, but then I have to go to the library."

"I can carry it," Anne said absently. She continued to stand looking at the kitchen as though she had been away decades instead of months. "Don't they wash dishes?" she asked finally.

Spencer glanced at the sink. "Well, it's different," he said. "It's bound to be." Then, "Look, do you want me to stick around? I can go to the library later."

"No, of course not. I have to unpack and then I'll probably take a shower or a walk or something."

Spencer started to speak, but instead picked up her small suitcase and started upstairs with it. "I'll be moving back in a day or so," he yelled. "Easier to study here than in the dorm."

She knew, of course, that he lived in the dorm, but she had been hoping that he might have moved home before she arrived. "Aren't you coming for dinner?" she asked when he came back into the kitchen.

He stopped, looked at her. "Sure, I guess I can," he said. "I'll be back by five."

Anne stood at the living room window and watched him pedal off toward the campus. "The Reluctant Dragon" was what her mother called Spencer's bicycle. Rusty and decrepit, it squealed at the stop sign on the corner. Then he turned the corner and disappeared.

Anne left the window and surveyed the living room and, through open doors, the study. She could see her father's desk, the leather chair where he read, her mother's wing chair, and the Chinese rug with its worn border of water lilies. For a moment she felt as though she had never been away and that nothing had happened.

She touched the yellowed keys of the piano and listened to the notes linger and fade. Out of tune. Nobody had bothered to have it tuned.

In the wake of the notes, the house seemed especially silent. Even the furnace, which normally banged all night at this time of year, was quiet. Anne played a handful of notes and turned away. She had to unpack.

The upstairs hall was dim. A little daylight filtered through the doorway from her room, but instead of going in, Anne went on down the hall and looked in Spencer's door.

The room seemed vacant despite the bulging shelves of books, the signs and posters Spencer had collected over the years. She stood on the threshold, transfixed, as always, by Spencer's ancient warning: she must *never* enter his room without permission. She never had.

Anne took a deep breath. Behind her lay her room, her suitcase, her unpacking. But at the far end of the hall—She turned and looked at the door there.

It was half open. She could see a strip of the old rose carpet beyond it. Hesitantly she walked toward the door, pushed it open, and saw, first, her own face—thin, winter-pale, and uncertain—in her mother's pier glass.

The mirror was old and speckled with dark spots. The frame was chipped (*Really it's too shabby to use, I suppose, but it did belong to your great-grandmother*) and then, beneath it, she saw her mother's dressing table on which a handful of brush rollers was untidily strewn. A crumpled stocking trailed from her mother's little swiveling stool.

Anne turned her head slowly, taking in the room. The four-poster bed with its pineapple finials, the armchair slip-covered in a faded rose print, the reading lamp. Her father's slippers were beside the bed. In the open closet Anne could see the sleeve of his beige tweed jacket. But in the Chinese vase on the bookcase, where her mother had kept eucalyptus leaves (*Their fragrance, Anne, is as elusive as memory*), there now were half a dozen dyed carnations.

Anne stood looking carefully, making herself look. This was reality, she told herself. This was what, in her absence, had happened. She said it that way to herself —formally, firmly—but there was nothing in the saying that commanded her belief. The room was still as familiar as her thumb, still her mother's room, however dreadfully altered.

Anne turned back to the pier glass, hunting reassurance in its speckled surface, but saw only her own unbelieving face. "Your mother has been dead for over a year," she said deliberately to her reflection. "Your father has remarried."

But the words had no reality.

Two

The few things Anne had packed took no time to put away. Among them was the old gray sweat suit she wore for running. Most of the girls at school who ran ran in shorts, even in winter, and came in with legs as red as blisters. But Anne, who was always cold, wore the sweat suit.

She stripped out of her blouse and skirt and put it on. The pants were short, not quite reaching her anklebones. Partly this was because they had shrunk, but mostly it was because she was so tall that it was hard to find pants long enough. She had been tall at twelve. Now, at sixteen, she was almost as tall as Spencer and almost as big-boned. She was, in fact, exactly her mother's height. She had her mother's coloring—dark red-blond hair and the pale skin that went with hair that color. "Anne is her mother's daughter," people often said, meaning the hair, the height, even the name Anne, which they shared. Eyes, too, and the shape of their noses. And yet it had always seemed to Anne that these features, so similar, were somehow better arranged in her mother's face. Her mother had been beautiful. Anne, looking at herself in the long mirror on the closet door, could by no means call herself that.

She tugged at the sweat suit and saw, as she always did, that any amount of tugging was futile. She sat down and pulled on a pair of socks.

Downstairs the ship's clock in the kitchen struck, and then the house was quiet again, quieter for the silvery sound of the striking. Without thinking much about where she would go, Anne put on her running shoes and a knitted cap. She found a pair of Spencer's old gloves in the back hall closet and let herself out the door.

The drizzle was cold, close to becoming snow. It clung in frozen drops to the sleeves of her jersey. Anne tested the pavement for slipperiness and started up Lincoln, jogging slowly at first to let her legs stretch.

This street, she thought, was where she had learned to play every childhood game she knew—kick-the-can, stoop tag, hopscotch, jacks. She had learned to ride a bicycle coasting down the small incline in front of the Mortimers' house, had learned to jump red-hot-pepper after school with Laura, and had skinned her knees on the sidewalk.

On one side of the street she had walked to school, walked home on the other, calling hello to old Professor Arnstein, loud enough so that he could hear even if his hearing aid was off.

Anne looked down at the wet sidewalk, dark under her feet. There must, she thought, be a million of her footprints impressed like ghosts somewhere in the concrete— hers and Spencer's, hers and Laura's, hers and, last summer, Eric's.

Hers and her father's. Anne looked up at the stop sign she was approaching. Taking walks was something they had liked to do.

She turned at the sign and headed toward campus, beginning to feel a rhythm start as her legs stretched and moved more easily. A dog stopped and barked at her, and she made a wide circuit around it because it was one she didn't know. Cars passed, making soft liquid sounds on the pavement. Bicyclists passed, heads down against the drizzle.

In another mile she wouldn't notice any of that. She had learned at school that for a mile or so she felt her legs, was aware of her breathing and the pumping of her arms. She heard sounds around her, noticed things. But after two miles it became automatic. Her legs ran, not because she commanded them, but because they had fallen into the rhythm of running. Sounds and distractions fell away. Gradually she stopped thinking. By the end of two miles she knew she would be only—mindlessly—running.

Anne cut across the rear lawn of the library, dodging students coming out the back doors.

At school she had discovered the forgetting that was part of the rhythmical movement. She had found that she could think of nothing at all while she ran and that afterward, sometimes for several hours, she remained forgetful, enclosed, as it seemed, in a shell of crystal. And so she had begun to run farther—five miles or six, farther some days—as far as she needed to.

October a year ago, on the day her father had called, she had run all afternoon—through the burning autumn fields, over rocks and stubble and into the woods, crunching on acorns. Miles. Until finally she was crunching nothing, feeling nothing but the rhythm in her legs. His news had become a heaviness lying beneath her ribs—a runner's pain.

She had carried it like that—a dense knot under her ribs—into the already lighted dormitory. Her roommate looked up from the desk where she was reading. "What's wrong with you?" she asked. "Did you talk to Crowell about the Latin quiz?"

And Anne, staring at the gooseneck lamp on the desk, realized that she would probably never tell her mother about the Latin quiz, would never have to disappoint her. She shook her head. "It's my mother," she said.

"Oh, no wonder. I get in a foul mood every time I talk to mine."

Anne looked at this stranger whom she had known so briefly. "I've got to go home," she said. And then, saying it for the first time aloud, "I'm going home. My mother is dying."

Now the drizzle had increased, but she ran on. She

glanced at the Chemistry building, passing it—lights in the labs, heads bending over tables. Then a kiosk encrusted with posters, the Anthropology museum, the bridge over the track—passing it all in drowsy rhythm. The steep hill rising to the lighted dorms, the entrance to the hospital. Houses again. Apartments. Dogs.

Running now almost without knowing she was running, she circled back through the drizzle and the twilight. She moved automatically, feeling the rhythm down the length of her body, from her shoulders to her hips and into her legs.

She passed along the edge of the campus, heard faint music, smelled onions frying, saw neon staining the pavement red under her feet as though she were seeing it from far away. From another place. Another time.

Finally again there was Lincoln Street, the stop sign, the Carmichaels' yellow house on the corner. Anne slowed and turned in.

She walked the last block, breathing deeply, looking at the familiar houses with their lighted windows, vague behind the curtain of rain. She had almost reached the house again before she remembered the two cups in the sink.

She stood dripping in the back hall, shook out the hat and mittens, and shivered inside her sodden jersey shirt. She could hear the sound of Spencer's recorder, the notes faint and faintly medieval, drifting down the stairs.

He was sitting at his desk playing something she'd never

heard before. On the floor of the room was his duffel bag. "What's that you're playing?" she said, standing on the threshold.

"It's a new thing we're working on." Spencer put down the recorder. "What'd you do? Go swimming?"

Anne looked down at the sweat suit so wet it was no longer gray but charcoal.

"Shouldn't you get that thing off before it gives you bronchitis?"

In her room she pulled off the sweat suit and found a pair of jeans and a sweater hanging in the closet exactly where she'd left them three months ago.

She gathered the clothes, put on a robe, and went down the hall to the shower. The water was like hot needles on her skin. Eyes closed, she groped for a towel, stepped out, and dressed. Then, barefoot, towel wrapped around her head, she padded back to Spencer's room. "Okay if I come in?"

Spencer nodded. He stood up and put a record on the stereo. Anne shivered, tucked the towel around her neck and sat down on the floor beside his bookcase, taking, without thinking, her usual place in the room. She listened to the opening bars of music. "Schubert?" she said.

"Good for you. The two-cello quintet."

"Do you still listen to Brahms?"

"Sometimes."

She remembered sitting beside his bookcase a year ago, fingering the spines of books, while Spencer listened to Brahms quartets. They hadn't known what else to do during that week while they waited for their mother to die. Anne pulled the rough terry cloth tighter around her neck. "What time do they get home?"

"Around six. I told you what Dad said."

She had forgotten.

"Annie, you don't have to worry. It's fine."

"I'm not worried."

"You're something. You don't look happy."

She regarded the books on the bottom shelf, arranged by no particular system as far as she could see. "Why should I be happy?"

"Why not? It's really better all the way around."

"Who's it better for?"

"For Dad. For Dory. For all of us really."

Anne bent to stare at the rug, tracing a figure eight in the nap with one finger. "What about Mother? Do you think it's better for her?"

"Mother's dead."

"But, my God, Spencer! He hardly waited a year!"

Anne traced the eight and retraced it, making it deeper in the nap of the rug. Spencer stood up. He put his duffel bag on the bed and began unpacking it—began dumping it, actually—the contents sliding off the bed onto the floor. "I thought you weren't moving back until the weekend," Anne said.

"Changed my mind."

She felt a lurch of gratitude. He'd decided to move home sooner because of her, she thought, but she said, "Are you just going to leave the stuff like that, in a wad?"

'Temporarily."

"This whole house looks like a bird's nest," she said.

Spencer sat down at the desk and rocked back in the chair. "Give it time."

"The house?"

"The situation. You'll be surprised, you'll like Dory."

"I *know* Dory."

"But you'll like her being here." Spencer rocked forward and pulled a cigarette out of his desk drawer. He lit it, taking his time, still rocking.

"Do you, Spencer? Do you like Dory being here?"

He squinted thoughtfully at the burning end of the cigarette. "Yes, I do," he said. "Quite a lot."

Anne sat up, feeling the whole length of her spine straighten. "How can you say that, Spencer? How can you be that disloyal to our mother?"

"I don't consider it being disloyal," he said.

She looked at him, and while she looked, he seemed to grow hazy behind the curling smoke of his cigarette. He seemed remote to her—distant in both space and time—as if he belonged to some time other than the one she occupied.

This strange, hazy Spencer leaned forward in the chair. "Have you talked to Laura?"

"I just got home."

"She called on—I guess—Sunday to see when you were coming. Also somebody named Eric, Dory said."

"Eric Borders."

"Who's that?"

Anne unwound the towel and pulled it off. "Someone I went out with last summer."

"I don't remember him."

"You weren't *here* last summer."

Downstairs a door slammed. The posters taped above Spencer's desk rippled in a draft Anne couldn't feel. "They're home," she said flatly, and stood up.

Three

She met her father halfway down the stairs as he started up toward her, calling her name. He held out his arms in welcome and hugged her, pressing her face against the rough fabric of his jacket. Tall as she was, she was smaller than her father, and her nose was buried in the curve of his shoulder. The smell of wool, cold air, and pipe tobacco was so familiar, so much his smell, that she caught her breath.

"Well," he said, holding her. "Well." And then he said it a third time as if the word were some sort of summary.

"I'm sorry I couldn't meet you," he said. "Was the plane on time?"

She nodded wordlessly.

"Tuesday's my long day. I hope Spencer explained."

"It was all right."

"Otherwise, of course, I'd have been there—" And she nodded again, feeling the jacket scratch her cheek like his morning beard when he used to wake her for school.

"Now let me look at you," he said. "Quite well, are you?" He held her at arm's length, and she sensed some beginning hitch of awkwardness in the motion. He smiled.

"You look fine. Your letters sounded that way." And then, carefully, after a minute, "Dory and I looked forward to your letters." Deliberately said, like a sentence he had been practicing.

In the light shining up through the banister spokes, he, like Spencer, looked remote to her, curiously distant. Tweed jacket, woolen tie, creased cheeks—all distant and strange. She pulled her arm away.

"Come downstairs and see Dory," he said gently, and because sooner or later she knew that she would have to, she followed him.

Dory was scurrying, stocking-footed, around the kitchen with a large apron tied over her sweater and skirt. Anne's first thought was how small she looked in this house where everyone was tall.

"Anne, welcome home!" She touched Anne's shoulder lightly, a quick bird tap, tentative and uncertain. "It's wonderful to see you. Wonderful to have you here."

Exactly, Anne thought, as if in a few months' time it was *she* who had become a visitor in the house.

"Was it a good trip? Are you tired out from your

semester?" Words bouncing like a beach ball on the slow waves of Anne's disbelief.

"Actually," Anne said, "we don't have semesters like the University. Ours doesn't end till January."

If she hadn't known Dory, seeing her working in the kitchen might have seemed less strange. But this was the same Dory Anne had known for years—small and plump, with curly reddish hair that was dulled by gray. Dory might be forty or she might be older. Anne had never wondered. She had been the secretary in the History Department for as long as Anne could remember, and now she lived in this house.

"I'm a very disorganized cook," Dory said apologetically. She looked at Anne over her shoulder. "My experience is mainly in TV dinners." Then she clattered the broiling pan out of the oven drawer. "But we're going to have steak?" She said it like a question, hopefully. "We thought you'd never have that at school."

"That's right. We never have it."

Anne's father went into the pantry and began making drinks, and Spencer came into the kitchen. "Is there any beer?"

"I hope so," Dory said. "I think I bought some."

"You think you're old enough for a beer?" he said to Anne.

"Legally?"

"Of course not legally, dumbbell. Spiritually."

"Oh, listen to him," Dory said. "What does that even mean—spiritually?"

"It means in her deepest self." Spencer flourished his can of beer. "It means in the depths where her soul resides."

"This family always sounds like books," Dory said. "Half the time, Anne, I don't know what they're talking about."

Anne looked from one of them to the other as if she had dropped into a stranger's house. Her father came out of the pantry. "Here." He handed Dory a martini. "Have a little something for where *your* soul resides." Smiling at her. Making a little joke. And again Anne was swept with disbelief, with a sense of betrayal.

It was like watching a play, she thought. No more real than that. They were actors putting on a homecoming scene. And she was the audience, sitting high up in the second balcony, reluctantly watching the fiction unfold.

At dinner there were candles—candles and steak and her mother's best Wedgwood plates, which they had almost never used when her mother was alive.

Anne cut her meat carefully and answered their questions. She described her courses and her teachers, explained the honor system to Dory, mentioned a paper she'd brought home to write. And eventually they began to talk of other things.

It *was* like a play, Anne thought, listening to them. The idea appealed to her.

She looked at her father—a little stooped, a little tired. A professor of medieval history, the stage directions would say. Slightly worn by the generations of students he'd taught, by the papers he'd read, and the doctoral committees he'd served on. Given to medieval references in his conversation and to jokes only graduate students understood. But, of course, that part would show up in the dialogue. Stage directions would simply describe him, would say, possibly, that the collar of his shirt was frayed and that the threadbare edge touched his neck at just the place where the skin wrinkled.

Anne looked away. Spencer was finishing a second helping. She had entirely lost the conversation.

She offered to clear the dishes, but Dory wouldn't hear of it on her first night home. So Spencer helped, and Anne sat with her father.

"It's good to have you home," he said. "I miss you."

Anne straightened the edges of her place mat with the tips of her fingers and recognized her mother's gesture. "Well, anyway," she said, "you have Spencer around."

After dinner she said that she was tired—and, in fact, she *was* tired. It seemed to her that being in the house was costing her terrific effort.

She tucked her few remaining clothes into bureau drawers and carried her toothbrush down the hall to the bathroom. In the sink there was a scatter of apricot powder. Abruptly Anne turned on both taps full force and waited until the water had flushed it down.

The house was still in the morning when she woke up. She looked at the clock and knew that all three of them had left by then. There was a lingering smell of toast in the air, and of coffee. Anne looked at the wall beside the bed, studying the wallpaper's narrow deep-blue stripes, troubled by the deceptive familiarity of the room. Then she stretched and pushed back the covers.

The kitchen floor was cold to her bare feet. She filled the teakettle and put it on the stove. While she waited for it to boil, she made herself think about the day. There were several things to do, but most important was the paper she had brought home to work on for English class.

Mrs. Liggett had given them a list of novels, any one of which they could write about, and Anne had chosen *Heart of Darkness*. Mrs. Liggett had said it was one of the more difficult books on the list, that it had to do with more than it seemed to and that Anne might find it hard going. But she had chosen it.

She'd read it three weeks before, curled in the library over a weekend. She had made some notes. But now she felt reluctant to begin.

She *had* to begin. Spooning instant coffee into a mug, Anne felt impatient with herself. Too often lately she had felt reluctant to do the things she knew she had to do. She would work on the paper for a few hours and later, around three o'clock, she would walk to the high school and meet Laura coming home.

After all, she thought, it was only a matter of beginning the paper. As soon as she began, her old pleasure in working with words would appear. It was in many ways the oldest and deepest pleasure she knew.

The kettle whistled. Anne poured water and stirred. Standing at the kitchen window, she sipped gingerly at the scalding coffee.

The sky was overcast. It might snow or, as easily, it might not. She rested her forehead on the windowpane and surveyed the backyard—soggy, bleak, and colorless. Bare lilac bushes crouched beside the porch, along the alley fence bare trees. The garage needed paint. Snow would improve the looks of things. And then she noticed that the roses hadn't been covered.

The rosebushes were always covered before Thanksgiving—mounded with leaves and capped with little Styrofoam cones. But this year they stood there, forlorn sticks in her mother's rectangular rosebed. Anne decided to cover them.

She dressed quickly, found her old down jacket and a pair of thick gloves in the back hall closet, thrown in with a random assortment of outgrown or outworn things that no one had bothered to give away. The Styrofoam cones were nested neatly at the back of the garage. Anne carried them out to the rosebed and stood there, already cold, trying to remember what her mother had done. There had always been a lot of leaves around for mounding the bushes, but now there were none that she could see.

She felt helpless, ridiculously inept. She'd helped with the roses often enough, but she'd never thought much about how it was done. Always there had been her mother, dressed in one of her father's old sweaters, speaking gently as she packed leaves expertly around the base of a bush.

Anne looked around the bare yard for leaves and, beyond it, to the Mortimers', raked equally clean. Eventually she saw that, at the bottom of the hedge that separated the yards, there were some leaves clotted among the branches.

On her knees, she began to pull handfuls from between the brittle sticks, filling a bushel basket slowly. When she had filled the basket, she carried it to the bed, dumped it, and returned to the hedge. She made half a dozen trips, clawing out leaves and dumping them, sodden, half-frozen, onto the rosebed.

Finally, satisfied that she had enough, she squatted down and began to mound the first bush. But, again, she was uncertain. How high should the bush be mounded? She sat back on her heels and frowned. Sunlight skidded across the bed and disappeared. It was important to do a good job.

Behind her a door slammed, and she turned to see Mrs. Mortimer standing on the porch next door. Anne waved a wet glove. "I thought it was you," Mrs. Mortimer called. "Welcome home, dear."

Anne stood up and brushed off her knees. Mrs. Mortimer had been her mother's best friend. "I got home yesterday," she called.

"Your father said it would be this week. I saw him in the bank." Mrs. Mortimer hugged her sweater around her and looked out over the rosebed. "I'm glad you're doing that," she said. "I worry about those roses."

"I guess nobody got around to them."

"Well, they really were your mother's pets, you know. And, after all, your father and Dory have so little time."

"My mother didn't have much time either." Anne could

hear her voice grow stiff, but Mrs. Mortimer had been distracted.

"Honestly, will you look at that feeder?" she said.

Anne looked at the bird feeder her father had built between the yards long ago. "It's all tilted again," Mrs. Mortimer said.

He had built it on a pole to discourage squirrels but somehow he had made it unstable so that a jay's weight could tip it and scatter the seed. "I'll straighten it," Anne said.

She could hear Mrs. Mortimer laughing behind her as she righted the platform. They had laughed when they first discovered the problem—her mother and Mrs. Mortimer. "He's like the White Knight in *Alice*," her mother had said, "blotting paper pudding and anklets to ward off sharks. Always some silly invention."

Anne gave it another tug for good measure. "That's better," Mrs. Mortimer called. "That'll last a few hours."

After Mrs. Mortimer went in, Anne knelt again to work on the roses. She piled leaves, fitted covers until she had completed a row. Then she straightened up to survey them. It was a ragged job. The covers weren't quite straight. Wet leaves straggled out from under them. It looked like the work of an eight-year-old, as flawed as the bird feeder. Anne sat heavily back on her heels.

She knew how they ought to look. She remembered the neat rows they had made in the thin November sunlight —done well, as her mother had done everything—and she started straightening the cones again, trying to make them look better.

Four

Laura's face broke into a smile and she started to run. "Hey, I was just on my way over to *your* house!" she shouted.

Anne watched her approaching, running down the sidewalk with a slipping armload of books, scarf trailing, disorganized as ever. Funny Laura never changed. She was—had always been—in a state of chaos.

Laura pulled up beside her, grinning. "You cut your hair," Anne said.

Laura pushed back her hair self-consciously. "I had to. She made me."

"Your mother?"

"Yeah. Writing her dissertation is turning her into a witch."

Laura began to rearrange her books. "One day I used up all the hot water washing my hair," she said.

"And Adele hadn't had her shower?"

"Right. And so Adele started yelling and Mother came flying out of the attic—I swear to God like she was riding on a broom—and screamed, 'That's it! You cut it!' Sometimes I wish she'd drop dead." And then Laura drew in her breath and clapped a frayed mitten over her mouth. "Oh, Anne, I'm sorry!"

"That's all right."

"Yeah, but I should have thought."

"Forget it."

Laura's small plump face looked stricken. "But you just got home!"

"What's that got to do with it? That's a non sequitur."

"A what?"

"Never mind."

Laura chuckled. "I'd forgotten how you talk." She shifted her books to the other arm and looked up at Anne. "You want to go down to Bank's and get some hot chocolate?"

It was a winter ritual—hot chocolate at Bank's—after ballet lessons, after flute, after a trip to the library, after anything that put them in the vicinity.

"Fine."

It was hot inside Bank's and smelled, as usual, of warm brown sugar. They found a booth near the back of the room, and Laura offered to get the hot chocolate. "For a treat," she said, "a welcome home."

"Do you have enough money?" And because Anne knew Laura never had, she reached into her pocket and pulled out some change.

She watched Laura walking to the counter, as small and round as Anne was tall. The hem of her coat was out in back and probably had been for months. There was something waiflike about Laura, Anne's mother had always said. She had called Laura "The Poor Little Match Girl."

When Laura returned with the hot chocolate, she had slopped some into the saucers. "Sorry I'm a klutz," she said placidly. "Want a napkin?"

Anne mopped up the chocolate in her saucer. Laura unwound her scarf and squirmed out of her coat. "Nothing has changed much at school," she said. "Corning's still a sadist. She's still giving me C's in English. Nothing much has changed in my social life either. No guys, in other words." Laura glanced up at Anne and smiled wryly. "My mother says my time's coming, but what does she know?"

"What happened to the guy you wrote me about?"

"Benjamin? Well, Benjamin's father got transferred to Los Angeles in November."

"Too bad."

"Yeah, well, maybe not so bad since Benjamin and I weren't exactly a heavy number. He never asked me out actually. This way I can always think he was about to."

Anne nodded.

"Have you talked to Eric?" Laura asked.

"He called before I got home."

"Oh." Laura nodded approvingly. "Are you excited to see him?"

Anne frowned. She wadded up the wet paper napkin and tucked it into her saucer. "I haven't really thought much about it."

"No?" Laura looked puzzled, but she went back to stirring her cocoa. "I suppose you've got a lot on your mind," she said.

"What do you mean?"

"Well, at home. It must be really different."

Anne took a careful sip of hot chocolate.

"I was totally surprised when your father got married. Weren't you?"

"Yes."

"I mean your mother was so—I don't know. Remember how we'd always sit on the stairs and listen to her play, and it sounded just like a record?"

Anne remembered. Afternoon sunlight on the open piano, and her mother's face, preoccupied with her music.

"So I never thought he'd marry again."

"But he did."

"I guess it's just natural," Laura said. "Everyone says she's a very nice woman."

Anne didn't reply. She sipped her cocoa and then they talked of other things—people they knew and what had happened during the fall. They finished their hot chocolates, and when Laura looked up, chuckling, Anne was startled at how vague and distant she had become.

They cut across the edge of the campus on the way

home. The buildings were dull in the dull December light. Someplace in one of them Spencer was sitting in his political science class. Across the campus in his dusty office, beneath the engraving of Rouen Cathedral, her father would be working on the book he never seemed to finish—and a few doors down the hall was Dory.

"I talked to Mr. Babbitt," Laura said. "I forgot to tell you. He says you can come to choir rehearsal if you want to. We've only had two rehearsals so far."

The two of them had sung in the church choir at Christmas Eve service for years.

"There'll be rehearsals every day next week," Laura said. "Like usual."

"I have a dentist's appointment Monday afternoon," Anne said doubtfully.

"So miss Monday. They're the same old carols, pretty much the standard stuff."

When they reached the corner where they went separate ways, they stopped.

"I think it would be nice if you'd come," Laura said. "Like old times." She looked up at Anne earnestly, put out her hand to touch Anne's sleeve. "You've had a couple of kind of weird Christmases."

Anne shrugged. "Anyway, I hope you will," Laura said. "I can see why you didn't feel like singing last year, but I didn't like it without you."

Anne began to back away from the corner. Laura hitched up her books and set off down the street. Anne watched her grow smaller, disappearing in the fading light, and thought of how many times she had stood there watching

Laura and how singing in the choir *would* be like old times. The carols were ones she'd always known, had learned by heart before she could read music, sitting curled beside her father on Christmas Eve while her mother played accompaniment on the piano.

She let herself into the house and paused in the hall. There was the sound of someone typing. Spencer? But almost at once Anne realized that it couldn't be Spencer. The steady tapping was too expert to be his.

Dory was sitting at a card table in the living room, silhouetted against the great uprising wing of the piano top. She stopped typing when Anne came in and smiled at her. "Busman's holiday," she said. "I came home early so I could type here instead of at the office."

"What are you typing?"

"An article for your father. One I've been trying to get around to for about a month."

Spencer was sprawled on the sofa with a book propped open on his stomach. "I thought you had class," Anne said.

"I cut it."

"You cut it yesterday, too."

"Different class."

"Is that your new policy? One a day?"

"Just today. To try to get the reading done before finals." Spencer shoved his glasses farther up on the bridge of his nose. "May I remind you that yesterday I was meeting a plane."

Dory had begun to type again, her fingers moving

swiftly on the keys. Anne sat down on the stairs and looked at the two of them, already absorbed again in what they had been doing. The typewriter made a sharp staccato in the quiet room, a kind of mechanical melody. Dory leaned forward to frown at the paper in the machine like someone reading music.

"I wonder if this could be right," she said. "Do either of you have any idea whether this sentence makes sense?"

She read them the sentence slowly, an elegant, convoluted arrangement of words that sounded, to Anne, exactly like her father.

"It makes *sense*," said Spencer, "but he could have said the same thing in a lot fewer words."

"Well, I knew it was good," Dory said. "I don't understand a word, but I can tell that. It's like listening to him talk. Half the time I don't know what he's saying, but I know he's right."

"How can you possibly know that," Anne said, "if you don't understand it?"

"She has a sixth sense," said Spencer.

Dory laughed and began to type again. Spencer snapped on the lamp behind him, and the light was reflected on the windowpane and on the shining mahogany wing of the piano. Anne stood up. "That's preposterous," she said. "There's no such thing as a sixth sense." She went upstairs.

The typing continued undisturbed, filling the upstairs hall with its steady cadence. Anne sat down at her desk and opened the notebook with the notes she had jotted down for her paper.

There were fewer than she had remembered making. They lay on the page in her neat, precise handwriting, seeming now to be the barest beginnings of ideas.

After a while she heard Spencer coming upstairs. He put his head in at her door. "What was that all about?" he said.

"What do you mean?"

"Just now. Downstairs. Why were you nasty?"

Anne closed the notebook. "That was a stupid thing to say—a sixth sense. As a matter of fact, you both said stupid things."

"What did Dory say?"

"About Daddy."

"That she can't understand everything he says? That's a crime? Who ever could?"

"Mother."

Spencer gave her a look she couldn't interpret. There were moments when she felt decisively the five years between them. She looked at him, tried to read his face, but his expression seemed folded in on itself like a smooth, complicated origami paper.

"Yeah," he said finally. "Well, this is a brave new world, my friend. You might try joining it."

Anne turned her back and, after Spencer had gone away, she opened the notebook again and tried to decipher the sentences she'd written. But what she saw was the expression on Spencer's face—bland and unreadable—as if he knew something that he didn't care to share.

She got up and walked to the window. The wind had blown one of the rose cones loose, and it tilted, like her father's bird feeder, askew in the straight-sided bed.

Downstairs, the typing continued, expert and unruffled—irritating. Anne found herself wishing that Dory would miss a note.

She lifted the heavy red-blond hair off her neck, piled it on top of her head, and stood looking at the twilight beyond the windowpane. She was separated from all of them by a pane of glass.

A brave new world, according to Spencer, as if he had forgotten the old one, when they had sung carols around the piano and their lives had been orderly and loving and content.

After dinner her father poked up the fire in the study and added a log. He turned to Dory, who was curled up, knitting, in the wing chair. "That's the last of the old apple logs," he said.

"That makes me sad," Dory said. "They smell so good burning." She stretched like a cat in Anne's mother's wing chair. "Let me see if this fits you," she said, holding up her knitting.

Anne's father laughed. "Sweetheart, scarves don't have to *fit*."

And then Dory laughed, embarrassed. "I guess I just want to see how it looks on you."

Anne turned away and watched the last of their old apple tree catch fire, licked by blue and eggshell flames. "I used to like to sit in that tree," she said slowly. "I used to sit in it and watch Mother and Mrs. Mortimer sew. They sat underneath it in the canvas lawn chairs. I sat in the branches. Mother usually was turning collars on your shirts." She said this looking steadily at her father, and he nodded.

"She often did that," he said calmly, as if, for him, too, this new world had swallowed up the rest.

Anne's bedroom seemed cold after the warmth of the fire. Shivering, she searched through the bureau for her old flannel nightgown and found it in the bottom drawer. Beneath it lay a tissue paper package. Through the paper Anne could see the sweater—deep blue, the color of hyacinths. She remembered the swift motion of her mother's needles as the wool gathered shape in her hands. Anne had forgotten tucking it away there. Still shivering, she closed the bureau drawer.

Five

Anne looked out at the yard. Weak afternoon sunlight slanted without warmth across the inch or two of snow that had fallen during the night. She looked back at the Conrad notes. Downstairs, the typewriter clicked rhythmically. Anne tried to ignore the sound. It had become more than an irritation by now. The steady, easy tapping of the keys seemed to mock her own halting efforts to understand the novel. She picked up the book and thumbed through it, as if that would accomplish something. She looked at the clock, watched the hand ease its way toward three-thirty, and frowned. When the telephone rang and Dory called her, Anne was glad of an excuse to get up.

It was Eric. She knew that sooner or later it was bound to be.

"I called before you got home," he said.

"Spencer said you did."

"And I'd have called last night except that we went to get the Christmas tree and it took hours. You know how that is."

Anne tried to picture his face and failed. Downstairs the typewriter clicked relentlessly. She closed her eyes, to shut out the sound, to remember the face.

"There's a party Saturday night," he said. "I may be able to have the car if it doesn't snow."

And she thought that, of course, he would have his license now. He, too, had turned sixteen in the fall.

"But if it does snow, probably not. They get nervous."

"They" was the way he had always referred to his parents, she remembered—as if they were a kind of anonymous force.

"It doesn't matter if you can't," Anne said. "We can walk."

"Like last summer," he said, and she looked at the jumble of phone cord tangled on the floor at her feet.

There was a pause. "It'll be nice to see you," he said, and she heard more than statement in his voice. He was asking her a question. He was wondering how she felt. She couldn't answer. It was as if Eric, too, had joined the world on the other side of the glass, remote from the one she inhabited.

She looked at the mouthpiece of the telephone, at the

small concentric circles of dots growing larger from center to periphery, and said, because she had to say something, "What time on Saturday?"

"Seven?"

She nodded and then realized that she hadn't spoken. Gathering herself from what seemed a great distance, she said, "It will be nice to see you, too." But the words were just words, without any meaning.

She replaced the receiver gently. Below, the typing continued like measures of music, expertly played, and suddenly Anne could no longer bear to listen. It seemed to her that as long as the sound filled the house she could concentrate on nothing else.

In her room she pulled on her sweat suit. "I'm going running," she said, leaning over the banister as she came downstairs. She let herself out the side door, crossed the yard, and went up the Lincoln Street alley, following the tracks the garbage truck had left in the snow. At the corner she turned east and headed for the river, glad to be running, glad to be out of the house that was loud with the sound of Dory's typing.

The wind stung her cheeks, and she bent against it. "It'll be nice to see you," he'd said, questioning. She had to think about Eric. He would ask directly how she felt when she saw him. It was only fair to try to reply because he would know—knew already—that she had changed.

Sliding on snow, she started up the gradual incline ahead, aware of her feet growing numb in her shoes. "Like last summer," he'd said. But it was not like last summer now. Last summer had been a time apart from the frozen months that enclosed it like parentheses.

She remembered windows open to the long twilights, moths beating against the screens in the study where she sat listening to her father reading Dante aloud. Warm evenings. June melting into July. She and Eric standing in darkness that was like velvet.

Anne had come home in June, apprehensive about spending a whole summer alone with her father. Spencer had left two weeks earlier to work in an orchard in northern Michigan. And so there would be just the two of them. She didn't know what that would be like.

Her father didn't know either. She could tell, riding home from the airport, that he had been wondering, too. "You'll be surprised at all I've learned to cook," he said.

"I suppose you'll need to buy a bathing suit and all that sort of summer thing," he said.

And then, as if it followed naturally from cooking and bathing suits, he asked, "Have you ever heard of Dante?"

Anne turned to look at him curiously. "Sure, I've heard of him."

"Have you ever read *The Divine Comedy*? I suppose not. Although I'm never sure what you and your mother may have read."

"Not that."

"Well, I've been thinking. How would you like for us to read it this summer?" As if that were the most logical thing on earth. It was a project he had devised for the two of them, she thought. Something they could do together.

And it touched her that he had been thinking about it, no matter how odd the choice seemed.

He had *The Divine Comedy* in paperback in three translations, but he chose a heavy leather-bound edition that cracked when he opened it. The first night home Anne pulled up the footstool beside his chair. He took out his glasses, lit his pipe, and then he began to read:

> "Midway in our life's journey I
> went astray from the straight road
> and woke to find myself alone in a
> dark wood—"

After that, most evenings they read, either in the study as they had begun or, on hot nights, on the porch until mosquitoes drove them in. All through June and into July.

Sometimes, while he was reading, the vertical lines in his cheeks deepened. Sometimes it seemed to her that his voice grew hoarse, and she thought that the words meant something particular to him at those times that she didn't understand.

For her, there was the old sorcery of words read aloud— words purely for the sound of them, for the feel of them in her mouth when she repeated them—words like smooth, melting pebbles. But there was also their meaning and the strange story they told of the man, Dante, who journeyed to the very darkest depths of Hell before he could begin to climb toward the light.

"It's an old journey," her father said. "I think perhaps we all take it sometime."

She nodded and listened to the words drift and merge, merge and separate and become one with the battering of the moths and the thin blue smoke rising from his pipe.

Toward the beginning of July they began to read the last part.

"It's the hardest part to understand," he said. "It's called the Paradiso, and it's tough. Do you have the courage to keep listening?"

Of course she had. So on a week of hot nights that followed hotter days, they began. They sat on the porch in the small circle of light the reading lamp made. Street sounds mingled with the words. Often Anne didn't understand. Sometimes the damp, sweet smell of the phlox along the porch distracted her. Those times she simply abandoned herself to the rise and fall of her father's voice and saw, in her imagination, strange wheeling images of light.

On one of those evenings Eric had called. She rushed into the house to answer the phone and was astonished. He asked her to go to the movies.

She came back to the porch, and her father looked up. "Was it for you?"

"Yes. I'm going to the movies Friday night."

"With Laura?"

"No. With Eric Borders. He's someone I knew when I was here in school." And had seen on the street a few days earlier. Still, she was amazed.

Her father looked at her quizzically over the tops of his

glasses. "It takes me by surprise from time to time to realize how fast you're growing up." It pleased her when he said that.

The movie was an old Woody Allen film that seemed to appear at one or another of the campus theaters every year. She had seen it before, but she never tired of seeing it. Afterward they bought ice cream. She remembered they ate the cones so slowly that they dripped on the way home along the streets that bordered the campus.

From the open windows of the rooming houses where the summer students lived had come music and laughter and the lonely notes of a single flute. From farther away came the bells of the carillon ringing the hour. The locust trees rustled overhead, and a plane droned. She remembered that he had held her hand.

He held her hand the rest of the summer. He kissed her. For whole long evenings they kissed each other, using movies or walks or ice cream as prologue. And she was happy, wandering the murmuring summer streets.

It seemed that the stillness inside her that had been there since her mother died was changing. A heaviness had begun to lift.

Late in July she told her father that she didn't want to go back to boarding school. He closed the book and relit his pipe, taking four or five matches and an interminable time to do it, and then he said, "Well, let's think about that. Your mother didn't think much of the high school here." Nothing else.

He hadn't insisted, had not really even argued, she thought. He had leaned against the porch rail, puffing his pipe, and she remembered that that was the first time he had mentioned Dory.

Anne took a deep breath of cold air. By August she had stopped wanting to stay home. By August, every time she turned around, there was Dory. When she leaned against Eric in the darkness, she wondered whether, at the same moment, Dory was sitting in her mother's house.

Arms pumping, legs churning, Anne ran, taking long strides as the hill grew steeper. The wind whipped a loose strand of hair across her face, and she brushed at it.

Eric's hair had smelled of cut grass. That was the last thing, at school, that she had kept remembering. After she could hardly remember how he looked, after she had stopped feeling much of anything at all, she remembered the smell of grass. And then, after a time, she only remembered remembering.

If she were to explain to him why she was different now, why, after she had promised to write, she had not written, that would be all that she could tell him—that sometime in August winter had begun again. It was all that she understood herself.

Ahead of her, tire tracks stretched uphill in the snow. Behind her, she imagined her own footprints strung out in ribbons. She reached the top of the hill and crossed over, started down, toes pushing numb against the toes of her shoes. The road slipped under her feet. The wind whipped the strings of her jersey. Through a gap in the trees she saw the river, then dropped below the gap and lost it in branches. A car passed, disappeared, leaving her a quiet stretch of empty road that led, just beyond the next bend, to the river.

At the bend she slowed, breathing hard, and jogged down the last small slope to the riverbank. It was warmer there. The trees on the opposite bank broke the wind. She could see the dam and the dam house a mile ahead. She began to run toward them.

It was more difficult running along the bank, breaking through the brittle stalks of summer weeds that jutted through the snow. She listened to the wind, hushed in the treetops, and thought of walking there with Spencer in the fall.

The ice on the river shone blue and violet in the late sunlight. Anne slowed her pace. She thought of the deep blue sweater in her drawer, the color of the ice, then of clicking needles and April rain.

"It's an excellent school, Anne." She remembered her mother's voice, gentle and persuasive, while the needles clicked, devouring blue yarn.

"But I don't really want to go away to school." She was sitting cross-legged on the rose rug in the bedroom.

The windows streamed with rain. The needles flashed. "I think you're making a mistake you'd regret. I've called the school, and we can visit." It seemed to Anne that the current of words was irresistible. Words about the school in autumn when the maples surrounding the hockey field were bright with fall color. Words about the funny skits at the graduation banquet. "Of course I imagine things have changed. But the maples will be there, and I can't think they'd ever give up the skits." Her mother had loved the school when she went there, and Anne was swept along on the current of her words.

She slowed to a walk, swatted at the withered stalks in the path. Oddly, she didn't remember exactly how they'd decided, but sometime during that rainy afternoon they had. Between them they had decided she'd go, while the hyacinth yarn wove itself into the sweater they packed in September at the top of her trunk. Packed it wrapped in the tissue that still contained it, never unwrapped, in the bottom bureau drawer.

The colors on the river had deepened. Sunlight streaked the ice. Close to the shore on the opposite bank a duck was floating on a still-unfrozen patch of water no bigger than a plate. There were patches like that all up and down the river where, as Spencer had told her once, the current moving underneath kept bits of water from freezing entirely.

Anne stood looking at the duck across the stretch of blue ice. She imagined the current still moving beneath the frozen surface, invisible but strong. Then, shivering inside the damp jersey, she turned back the way she'd come and began to run again.

Six

She climbed the hill from the river under arching bare branches. She was tired. Her legs ached. They had not stopped aching, she realized. And she had not stopped thinking. All that running—five miles at least—had failed to have its usual anesthetic effect. She was surrounded by memories. It was being home, she thought. It was the colors on the river. It was the deceptive familiarity of things that were no longer the same. Jogging more slowly, she started down the hill.

It had never occurred to Anne that her father would want to marry again. Certainly she had never thought of Dory, who was as unlike her mother as anyone she could imagine.

When he had called her at school early in November to tell her, not that it was going to happen, but that it already had, she remembered looking at the telephone's dial blankly, seeing the numbers enclosed in the little black circles distinctly, but hearing only vaguely what he'd said. "Dory?" she'd said finally, and had found she could say nothing more.

That call matched the other—a year before—that had brought Anne flying home because something had exploded in her mother's head—a blood vessel had ruptured—and she was, unbelievably, dying. The calls were like bookends, bracketing the year.

She had run all that afternoon, run until the news became a stitch in her chest, no more real than words repeated interminably seem real. When she had run herself into exhaustion, she sat on a fence overlooking a field of stubble and thought about her mother.

Tall and gentle, sitting erect at the piano, playing Chopin; on her knees beside her perennial border, dividing phlox; writing letters at her desk in the bedroom while Anne lay beside her on the floor, doing arithmetic. Her mother's skin had been the texture of magnolias. She had run for the school board and won. She had entered figure skating competitions and won them. She had written poetry that was published in the *University Quarterly*. There was nothing her mother couldn't do except, in the end, stay alive.

In the first days after her mother died, the house, ironically, had seemed to come alive again. The telephone rang. Flowers were delivered. There were visitors. The house seemed almost to welcome the change, but, the week before, waiting, Anne had grown accustomed to stillness.

Her grandmother arrived from Racine, like a broom intent on sweeping out cobwebs. Blue waved hair tucked into a hairnet, she alternately worked and wept. She put flowers in vases, emptied the closet in the bedroom, and then, like a balloon losing air, collapsed into a chair, weeping. Anne sat, some days, locked in the bathroom to escape her.

After the funeral more people came. Ellen, who had worked for them for years, put ice and whiskey in the living room and answered the door. Spencer stuck around, shaking hands, but Anne closed herself in her room and listened to the voices and the clink of glasses that sounded curiously like a party. She wanted to be away from the touching that people felt obligated to do.

It was mild October weather, but, to her, it felt like winter. The next morning, waking, she was surprised to see warm Indian summer sunlight in the yard where she had half-expected snow.

She remembered brushing her hair in the bathroom, saying tentatively to her reflection, "Your mother is dead." The face in the mirror had returned her look blandly, and so she tried again—slowly, deliberately repeating the words. The reflection remained impassive, refusing to hear.

She had put her hand on the cold glass of the mirror as if

she were trying to touch the face there, but the reflection lay beneath the surface of the glass, untouched and untouchable as a brown leaf frozen beneath the ice of a lake in winter. And so she had scooped her hair back in a rubber band and gone down to breakfast.

Spencer and her father sat reading newspapers, drinking their coffee. "Do you want to take a walk when you're through?" Spencer asked her.

"Where?"

He shrugged. "Anywhere. Dad's going down to the office for a few hours this morning."

They had walked to the river. The carillon was ringing. Scatters of maple leaves blew down in bright gusts around them. She looked at her brother, trying to see how he was feeling.

"It feels different than you think it will, doesn't it?" she said.

"How did you expect it to feel?"

Anne paused. "I guess I didn't know. I thought maybe she'd get better." And that was true. Although nobody had given her any reason to hope, she had not imagined —could not allow herself to think—that her mother would let herself die.

Spencer said nothing for a while. They walked in silence through the falling leaves. "I think I got used to the idea sometime last week."

"How did it feel?" She needed to know. And, again, Spencer was quiet.

Presently he said, "I felt I was dropping deeper and

deeper until I kind of bottomed out. That's the best I can tell you."

Anne nodded, but she didn't understand.

They stood side by side looking at the slowly moving river. Ducks slid downstream, riding on the current, mirrored upside down in the sluggish water.

Anne broke off a willow twig and rolled it between her fingers, feeling its smooth, tender bark. "Spencer," she said hesitantly, "I haven't even cried yet."

She cried only once.

In the week before she went back to school, Anne sometimes forgot, coming into the house, that her mother was not there. She would open the side door, almost convinced that she'd hear the piano—the Chopin nocturne her mother loved—and would hear, instead, the sound of Ellen's radio in the kitchen.

Ellen had agreed to come more than her usual half day for a few weeks, and Anne liked to stay near her, hanging around the kitchen while Ellen ironed or cleaned vegetables.

"Why not call a friend?" Ellen would say. Or, "Don't you have schoolwork you should be doing?"

But Anne didn't want to call a friend or go upstairs into the silent hall. The faint odor of scorch, the droning of the radio were comforts beyond which stretched wintry spaces. She preferred to sit on the kitchen stool watching Ellen expertly flip a shirt collar and iron the reverse.

And then one afternoon Ellen looked up, startling her. "I miss your mama," she said.

Coming just that way, abruptly, the words caught Anne off guard and she felt them as a kind of blow.

Ellen flipped the shirt off the board and reached for a hanger. "She was a saint of a woman," she said. "There wasn't anything she did but it was perfect."

The words seemed to prick the warm air between them. Ellen put the iron down on end, and Anne, looking at the flattened reflection of the stove on its flat surface, heard Ellen sniff. She looked up, appalled to see tears in Ellen's eyes. "Don't," she said sharply. "Don't do that, Ellen." But the tears overflowed. Ellen began dabbing at her cheeks. "I said *don't!*" Anne shouted, and suddenly she couldn't stand it. She jumped up and fled the room, terrified.

The kitchen door swung shut behind her. She started upstairs. She felt as though something were cracking inside her. She leaped the stairs as if she were in danger of falling through.

In the upstairs hall she paused, breathed, pressing her hand against the pain beneath her ribs. Her breath splintered in her chest.

At the end of the hall was the door to the attic. Its knob reflected cold light. Anne walked toward it slowly, hugging her ribs, and slowly turned the knob, easing back the latch until the door opened. She climbed the stairs, and, hesitating, she turned on the light.

At the far end of the attic, hanging from a rafter, stark in the light of the overhead bulb, was a quilted plastic garment bag. In it were the dresses her grandmother had saved. Too good to give away. Her mother's dresses.

For a time Anne stood looking across the bare board floor, past the cartons and boxes stacked along the walls. And then tentatively, as if she were approaching a deep mystery, she crossed the room and, with fingers that trembled, worked down the bag's zipper until the dresses were exposed to the glaring attic light.

From downstairs Ellen's voice called her. She could hear the wind in the eaves and her own breath coming unevenly. Her hands shook. Timidly she reached into the bag and touched a fold of cloth. And then, with a sound she did not at first recognize as her own, she threw her arms around the clothes and plunged her face into an armload of fabric.

Beneath her ribs the pain exploded in bursts that seemed all light and sharpness—rockets of pain, starbursts, spreading upward into her throat, choking her. With a great tearing feeling, she began to sob. She stood there sobbing, face hidden—hiding herself the way a child does, hurt and terrified, against its mother's skirt.

She stood—how long?—vomiting sobs like sickness, burying her face in cloth, ripped with feelings she couldn't even name.

And over and over she heard her voice saying, "I'm sorry. I'm sorry," as if somehow everything that had happened were her fault.

She cried until she was weak from crying, shaking as a child does after a fever. And then she closed the bag.

Afterward she splashed water on her eyes, refusing to let Ellen beyond the locked bathroom door. Through the door Ellen spoke to her gently, calling her baby names, saying she understood. But Anne was silent and kept splashing water. She knew Ellen couldn't understand. Anne couldn't understand herself. She thought of her grandmother weeping limply into a wadded handkerchief. It hadn't been like that. It had been fury, terrifying. White light. Screaming. A screaming inside her that was louder and higher than any actual noise could be. So loud, so high that it became not sound but light.

After that she had never gone to the attic again. She had tried and mostly succeeded in forgetting that day. It hadn't happened again. It would never happen another time.

Seven

Friday. She was having lunch with Spencer. He had invited her to meet him at noon as though she were not merely a younger sister but a friend.

It was ironic, she thought, that so often she got what she badly wanted only after it no longer mattered. Three years ago she would have run all the way from home to meet Spencer, astonished to be invited and afraid to be late. Now she very nearly *was* late, but she walked.

He was waiting for her outside Robbins Hall, lounging against one of the columns that supported its pseudo-Roman porch. As she crossed the street, Anne could see that under his jacket he was wearing the red plaid shirt she had given him three Christmases before. She remembered buying it—beautiful wool plaid and much more than she could afford. But she had wanted him to have it.

He shoved off from the pillar and came to meet her. "I was holding my breath, wondering if you'd show," he said dryly.

"I told you last night I was coming."

"Oh, but you've become so mercurial one counts on nothing."

"Shut up, Spencer."

"Where do you want to go?" he asked. "There's a new natural food place that's pretty good. Or would you rather go to Jack's?"

And, again, the fact that Spencer was willing to take her to Jack's, where his friends went, would have delighted her three years ago. "The natural food place, I think," she said. "Or is it all sprouts?"

It was like a greenhouse, full of hanging baskets of asparagus fern. There were white plastic tables and the menu on a chalkboard. They ordered leek soup.

"This is nicer than Jack's," she said.

"Healthier, too. I figure one meal in here counteracts a week of bad habits."

Anne moved her napkin so that the long-haired waitress could put down their bowls of soup. Spencer looked at the waitress, and then he looked at the soup.

"So how's it going?" he said.

Anne shrugged. "It's going."

"Nice seeing Laura?"

"Sure."

"Did that Eric fellow call?"

"You know he did. I told you."

"I'd forgotten."

"Well, he called."

"So how was it? Talking to him, I mean."

Anne put down her spoon. "What is this, Spencer, the third degree? It was okay. We're going to a party on Saturday."

"That's good."

"Why good?"

"He's a nice guy, isn't he?"

Anne nodded.

"So that's good."

She stirred her soup, raising small chunks of potato to the surface.

"You don't seem particularly interested in the whole project," Spencer said.

She looked at him, but the light from the window reflecting on his glasses made mirrors of the lenses.

"Are you?"

"Spencer," she said, "do you want to cut it out?"

"I didn't know I was bothering you."

"You are, though."

Spencer broke a breadstick into his soup. "You know," he said, and he said it slowly, which was the way he always said things when he was serious, "you've changed in some way, Anne. There's something different about you."

"I'm older."

"Something besides that." He paused. "You're having a rough time with all this, aren't you?"

"If by 'all this' you mean Dory, I wouldn't say it was a rough time. I'd say I'm not quite as crazy about her as you are."

"It isn't a matter of being crazy about her. She's just a fact. She's there."

Anne looked at him and tried to remember how it had felt when she wanted so badly to buy him the shirt, but all she could see were his glasses, opaque, reflecting light.

"I mean why not come to terms with it?" he said. "It's been a while."

"Someone has to remember Mother," she said.

He took a deep breath—exasperated, she knew, but she didn't care. "Nobody's *forgetting* her! But life does go on. Getting on with your life doesn't mean forgetting Mother."

But it did. It seemed to mean exactly that. They were all so intent on getting on with their lives that they seemed scarcely to remember her mother at all.

After a minute Spencer said, "You know what, Anne? It's like you're surrounded by a moat."

She shoved her half-empty bowl to one side. "Spoken like a true medievalist's son," she said.

"See what I mean? I can't get to you."

Anne picked up a breadstick and began crumbling it on the table. "Did it ever occur to you that maybe I don't want to be 'got to'?"

She felt suffocated by Spencer. She rolled the breadstick between her fingers. "I don't see how you can accept it," she said. "If you remember anything about how it used to be at home, I don't see how you can accept this. You must not remember."

Spencer glanced up from his soup. His face had the same folded expression that she had seen two nights ago. "I remember," was all he said, and Anne felt the same stirring of discomfort that she had felt then.

"Well then?" she said.

"I sometimes wonder what *you* remember," he said, and continued to eat his soup.

He ate with the same single-mindedness with which he approached everything. She watched the leisurely journey his spoon made from bowl to mouth and back again as if she were staring at a hypnotist's watch. "What do you mean?" she said, but Spencer kept methodically spooning up soup, and she didn't ask again.

She would have liked to be running. She imagined running while Spencer ate. She imagined landscape spread beneath her feet like a map and her legs, moving easily, carrying her away from the discomfort feathering at the edges of her mind.

"That's all you're going to eat?" he said, tipping his bowl for the last bite, and she nodded. "Okay," he said. "Then let's go."

She stood at the cashier's counter while he paid for their soup. They turned up their collars against the wind that had become colder in the hour they were in the restaurant. "Where are you going now?" Anne said.

"To the library, I guess. You want to walk that way?"

She matched her long stride to his and felt comfort in moving. "Sorry if I bugged you," he said after a while. "But you're on my mind."

Anne dug her hands into the pockets of her coat. "I've told you before, you don't have to worry about me, Spencer. I can handle things."

If you leave me alone, she thought. If everyone will just leave me alone. She looked up at the silver swags strung holiday-fashion between the streetlights, flashing in the cold sunlight like spangles of ice. What she wanted was to be left alone with what she remembered until the vacation was over and she could go back to school.

Mrs. Mortimer knocked on her kitchen window as Anne turned down the driveway. She waved. Anne waved in return, but Mrs. Mortimer wanted something else. She struggled to push up the storm window, finally came to the back door. "Do you have a minute, Anne? I want to show you what I've found."

Anne nodded and made her way across the yards, breaking through the crusted snow. At the end of the yard two jays jostled one another for space on the feeder. "A smart bird would just wait underneath until it tipped," Mrs. Mortimer said, arms folded across her chest for warmth. Then she squealed. "And it just did!" The jays flapped, startled, in midair. Seed scattered.

"Shall I fix it?"

"No, come on in. We can do it later."

The kitchen was warm and sunny and had its own

peculiar odor—part coffee, part Murphy's oil soap. On the counter there was a pile of photographs. Mrs. Mortimer gestured toward them. "That's what I want to show you. I've been sorting out drawers, and I found all these. I thought you might like to have some of them."

There were at least two dozen pictures on the counter, snapshots taken more or less recently. "Sit down and look," Mrs. Mortimer said. "I'll get you some coffee."

She put a cup down beside Anne and sat down herself. "Don't you want to keep these?" Anne said.

"A few, yes. But I thought I'd let you choose first."

Steam rose from the cups. Mrs. Mortimer passed her a little blue bowl of sugar and leaned over to look at the pictures with her.

They were snapshots of backyard picnics, family parties, one of Mrs. Mortimer and Anne's mother leaning against the apple tree. There were pictures of Anne and Spencer taken at various ages.

"I can't believe I ever wore my hair that way," Mrs. Mortimer said. "I think I wanted to look like Katharine Hepburn."

Anne smiled, looking at the picture of the two of them, so serious, under the apple tree.

"And you see? Spencer's tent." Mrs. Mortimer helped herself to sugar. "I'll bet you'd forgotten that tent."

"No. I remember. He put it up under the lilac bush, and the grass turned yellow underneath."

It had been his clubhouse. His and Max Taylor's. She remembered sitting by the hour on the back steps, hoping

—but not expecting—that they would let her join.

"And your mother," Mrs. Mortimer said, "in that red print skirt your father brought her from Boston. An Indian print."

Her mother was posed, smiling shyly, beside the front porch. But annoyed, despite the smile, as she always was when someone wanted to take her picture.

"That funny picture," Mrs. Mortimer said. "Your mother claimed your father was trying to turn her into a flower child." Mrs. Mortimer chuckled. "You wouldn't remember flower children. That was the early seventies around here." And then she sighed. "I miss your mother."

Anne nodded and picked up another snapshot. "Look— the feeder," Mrs. Mortimer said. "That goes back a while."

And there was her father, standing beside the feeder with a hammer in his hand.

"He didn't know its problem yet. He'd just driven the last nail." Mrs. Mortimer laughed. "You know I don't think he really cared much when he did find out. He just liked building it."

"Didn't he ever try fixing it?"

"Oh, maybe. I don't remember. He isn't the perfectionist your mother was. *She* may have tried. That's entirely likely."

Her father was smiling and squinting at the camera. She remembered when he had looked like that, years before, swinging down off the train steps at the station in Wisconsin, coming to spend a week of vacation with them at her grandmother's house. She remembered racing toward him, braids flying, glad that it was August, glad that he had come to join them at the lake. She remembered his catching her in midair. "You're bigger! You're so brown! When did your hair get long enough to braid?" And then, happily, looking beyond her, "Where's Mother? Where's Spencer? I've missed you three."

"He wasn't very old," she said now to Mrs. Mortimer. "Maybe thirty-three or -four. You were tiny."

"I was eight," Anne said, not sure why she knew that with such certainty.

She sorted through the photographs slowly, strangely disturbed. In all the pictures they looked so young, so invulnerable, so happy—as if nothing bad could ever touch them.

"What about this one?" It was a picture of them all, her family and the Mortimers, gathered at the Mortimers' dining room table.

"That must have been Christmas," Mrs. Mortimer said.

"No, Thanksgiving. You can tell by the chrysanthemums."

"Where's my mother?" The rest of them were there with their invariable smiles. Spencer, looking half choked in a necktie. She, herself, in her plaid wool party dress and braids.

"Let me see." Mrs. Mortimer squinted at the snapshot, turned it over to look for a date on the back. "She must have been in the kitchen," she said. "I can't think which Thanksgiving this would be."

When they had gone through all the photographs, Mrs. Mortimer offered her more coffee. Anne shook her head.

"I'm meeting Laura in about an hour," she said. "We're going Christmas shopping."

"Some things never change, do they? I can remember you and Laura shopping when you could barely see over the counters." Mrs. Mortimer stood up and gathered the cups. "What are you getting everyone?"

"Records, I guess. They like those."

"Dory too? Is she musical?"

Anne hesitated. She hadn't thought about buying a present for Dory.

Mrs. Mortimer put the photographs Anne chose into an envelope and wished her good shopping. Anne waded back across the yards to the house.

She looked at the snapshots again before she went out to meet Laura. She had chosen the one of Spencer and his tent, the one of her father with his hammer. She had chosen the Thanksgiving picture. She stopped brushing her hair and looked at it again, frowned. If her mother was in the kitchen, why was there no empty place at the table?

Eight

Laura was waiting outside Marshall's between the tables of discounted books that were always there under the overhang. Anne made her way up the street toward her through crowds. She dodged shoppers hurrying along, grimly clutching lists.

"I saw a lady club her kid just now," Laura said. "That's what I like about the Christmas spirit. Everyone's so relaxed."

They went first to the record shop so Anne could buy her presents. The store was hot and bright and full of people jostling each other for space near the bins of records. The floor was wet with slush. Anne squeezed her way to the bins, found the Mahler she had decided on for

Spencer, the madrigals for her father, and went to stand in line at the cash register. That left Dory.

"What are you going to get her?" Laura asked.

Anne moved forward with the line. She shook her head.

"You want to go get Adele's present then?" Laura said. "Maybe it'll come to you."

They crossed the street to the only department store in that part of town, and while Laura sorted through scarves and grumbled about spending money on Adele, Anne wandered down the aisle, looking into glass cases. There was every sort of thing to choose from—gloves, handbags, jewelry, cologne. She hadn't any idea what to buy. She had no notion of what Dory might like. Actually—and she stopped to consider the thought—she had no idea who Dory *was*. Dory was like a negative—an indistinct figure, gray on black film, who might have been almost anyone at all.

When Laura came trudging up with her package, Anne was still leaning against the stationery counter. "I got Adele a scarf," Laura said, "but I got a small one. How about you?"

"I'm trying to think," Anne said. "I can't decide."

"I think we should get something to eat," Laura said. "That usually helps." It seemed as good an idea as any.

Outside the store they pulled on their mittens. Squinting into the bright, slapping wind, they dodged their way through the shoppers and headed for Kresge's.

Anne led the way down the narrow aisle to the food

counter. Laura hitched herself onto a stool, and they tucked their packages at their feet. "Remember when we stole the lipstick here?"

"No," Anne said.

"You forget the funniest things."

"Are you sure it was me?"

"Of course. It was both of us. I nearly got murdered."

Anne glanced over her shoulder at the counters of lipstick and powder, the racks of mascara. She had no recollection of ever having done such a thing. "Why did we?" she said.

"To use when we played dress-up. Don't you remember how we clomped around in high heels pretending we were our mothers?"

The red print skirt that had hung to her ankles. The one her father had brought from Boston. The skirt in the photograph. Of course she remembered.

"I thought my mother would kill me when she found out," Laura said. "Don't you remember how we had to take it back and confess?"

Anne shook her head. She picked up the laminated plastic menu propped between the sugar and salt. "Now *your* mother," Laura said, and paused. She wrinkled her forehead. "You know, I can't remember what your mother did. I don't think she ever found out."

They ordered and sat watching their hot dogs turn on the grill that rotated slowly around and around. Anne stared, hypnotized by the movement. "Laura, why didn't my mother ever find out?"

"Oh, Lord," Laura said, "how can I remember? After all, we were only eight."

Within sight of the house Anne remembered the Christmas tree. They'd agreed to go buy it as soon as Dory and Anne's father were home from work, and they were home. Anne could see her father clearing ice off the porch steps. She began to run.

Dory was perched on the porch rail watching, bundled up like a child sent out to play. From that distance they could have been anyone, could even have been Anne, herself, and her father years ago, clearing the steps. Shoveling was something she had done with her father, following after the shovel's track, sprinkling salt from a paper bag.

Dory waved, and her father straightened up and watched Anne running toward them. "We thought you'd forgotten us," Dory called.

Going for the Christmas tree was an occasion, the first in a series, marking the beginning of the season. Like everything about their Christmases, buying the tree had been a lovely event and always the same. Riding across town to the Kiwanis lot, where they had always gone, Anne felt, in spite of herself, some of the old excitement.

Light bulbs were strung across the lot on poles. They swung in the wind, dappling the stacks of trees with crazy leaping patterns of light. Climbing out of the car, Anne smelled for the first time the deep, mysterious odor of Christmas. She wandered down the corridors of trees behind Spencer and the others, breathing the scent of pine and spruce.

A man dressed in heavy boots and gloves was leading them, holding up trees for them to inspect, shaking down branches. "You know," Dory said to him, "I haven't bought a tree for about thirty years. I was just a teenager when we stopped having them at home."

The man took this seriously. He looked at her sympathetically. "Everyone needs a Christmas tree," he said, and dug out a plump Scotch pine for her to look at.

Farther down the row Spencer was holding up a short-needled fir, which was the sort of tree they usually bought. "This looks like a pretty good one," he said.

"The trunk's crooked," said Anne. "Look at the top of it." She dug her hands into her pockets and looked around the lot for her father.

He was standing at the far end of the row where the tallest trees were always stacked—the "hotel lobby trees," her mother had called them. He was balancing an enormous spruce with one hand. "I think this is it," he called to her. She walked toward him.

"It's too tall," she said. "It won't possibly fit into the living room."

"Well, I think it just might."

Dory and the tree man came down the aisle of trees toward them. "It won't," Anne said to Spencer. "He'll have to cut a lot off the bottom and that'll ruin it."

"He likes big trees," Spencer said. "He always wanted our trees to be bigger."

"What makes you think that?"

"He said so. Don't you remember how every year he'd want to buy a great big tree?"

Anne shook her head. She didn't remember. "All I remember is that our trees were wonderful," she said.

They stood in a ring around the enormous tree her father had chosen. The tree man stood by patiently, beating his gloved hands against his sides. "Biggest tree on the lot," he said.

"It's beautiful," said Dory. "It's what you dream a Christmas tree will look like."

"It seems to me that someone who hasn't had a tree for thirty years ought to have an especially nice one," Anne's father said.

"Well, that's nice," Dory said. "That's beautiful."

Anne turned away. At the end of the row another family had begun propping up trees. Beyond and around them the light bulbs danced. She could barely make out their car on the street beyond the lot.

Their Christmases *had* been perfect. Spencer was wrong. Their father *had* always liked the trees they chose. Uneasily Anne examined the fingers of her glove. She felt a curious shifting doubt, a quicksilver movement that was there and then was gone. She turned again to look at the tree. She could see they would have to rope it to the roof of the car to get it home.

"Isn't it the way you *imagine* Christmas?" Dory said happily, nestling herself into the front seat after the tree had been roped to the top.

Spencer and her father climbed into the car. "It cost a

small fortune," her father said, but he seemed happy, too.

He turned on the ignition. The car coughed and died, coughed and died until it finally started. "Miserable car," he said peacefully, easing it into reverse.

"But it started," Dory said, "and it's Christmas—a great big tree and snow and all. It's like that song, you know— 'Over the river and through the woods—'."

"It isn't." Anne said it so sharply that both Dory and her father turned.

"You mean no horse," Dory said quickly. "No sleigh."

"Just our good old unreliable car," Spencer said. As if the two of them were trying to sew on a patch.

"That song has to do with Thanksgiving," Anne said lamely.

"Oh, maybe so," said Dory. "I've probably got it wrong."

She had it wrong. Anne was pretty sure of that, but the words of the song kept spinning in her head nevertheless. Spun and disturbed her. Troubled her and spun.

The tree was, of course, too big. The three of them stood crestfallen in the living room after they had dragged it in and propped it up and found that it was a good foot too tall. "The trunk's going to be too big for our stand, too," Spencer said.

"We'll just have to cut some of the trunk off and build it a stand," her father said. "I'll have some time to do it later in the week."

And then, Anne thought, it will look like Laura's haphazard trees and nothing like the pretty trees she remembered. She could imagine her mother standing in the room that minute, shaking her head and smiling ruefully at the silly situation. But, of course, her mother would never have let them buy such a tree in the first place. She would have talked them out of it.

Nine

"Joseph Conrad's hero, Marlow—" Anne crossed out "hero" and substituted the word "protagonist." "Conrad's protagonist, Marlow, journeys to the heart of darkness." She glanced at her notes and scratched the whole sentence.

It was true that Marlow traveled up the Congo into the heart of Africa, into the unknown, but there was more to it than that. Mrs. Liggett had as much as said so.

Anne sipped the coffee that had grown cold in the cup beside her on the desk. The roar of the vacuum cleaner downstairs distracted her.

"The journey into darkness can be interpreted several ways," Mrs. Liggett had said. Anne bit the end of her pencil. "It's an old journey. I think perhaps we all take it sometime." But these words were not Mrs. Liggett's. They were her father's, on the porch in the summer as they began to read Dante. And then, as if there weren't distractions enough, the words of Dory's song began to spin in her head. "Over the river and through the woods to grandmother's house we go—" Anne put down her pencil and stood up.

It was Saturday morning. Dory was vacuuming. Spencer was playing his recorder. Her father was talking on the telephone in the hall. No wonder she couldn't concentrate. A person would have to be deaf to concentrate in this house, she thought, and, rather than try, she decided to walk over to Laura's.

She was guiltily glad to leave the paper. The reluctance she had begun to feel about writing it earlier in the week was still there. She breathed the cold, uncomplicated air on Lincoln Street with relief.

The Dewitts' house, like most of the faculty houses near the campus, had seen better, more elegant days. Anne rang the bell and waited, tracing with one finger the frosted arabesques etched on glass panels in the front door. Inside the house, one of the Dewitts' dogs began to bark. Laura opened the door. The dog kept barking. "Don't mind her," Laura said. "She's pregnant."

From somewhere in the house came Mrs. Dewitt's voice, shouting to Laura to let the dog out. Anne looked around. On every flat surface there were, as usual, the Dewitts' overflowing card files—teetering precariously in small towers on the stairs, spilling onto the dining room table, stacked on the window seat and piled on an ironing board standing, apparently permanently, in the front hall. Laura followed her eyes. "My mother's two-thirds through with her damned dissertation," she said, "but my father's starting a book. There's no peace." She showed the dog through the front door and closed it. "I'm making tomato soup," she said. "Want some?"

Anne followed Laura into the kitchen and watched while she ladled soup into two chipped bowls. "Anyway, Adele's gone. That's one good thing. She won't be home until tomorrow."

"You can use up all the hot water," Anne said.

Laura put the bowls on the table and got out a box of crackers. "What I thought was, I'd mess around with her eye makeup."

"What for?"

"Because it's a great opportunity. She's such a miser she won't let me touch it when she's home."

Anne looked at her soup. There were small islands of undissolved tomato floating on the surface. Weak sunlight fell across the scarred surface of the table, across a drooping philodendron, withering in its pot. "So do you want to try it?" Laura said. "After we eat?"

"Won't Adele miss it?"

"I don't see how. She's got tons."

It was true. There was a vast supply—a whole drawer full of sticks and tubes which Laura scattered at random on the bureau. "Help yourself," she said. "There must be about a thousand dollars' worth of stuff here."

The room was a shambles. Laura shared it with Adele, and, between them, they had managed to fill every available space with their belongings. Anne looked for a place to sit. "Just shove things over," Laura said, and leaned forward to study her face in the mirror. Anne watched as she began to draw a black line along her upper eyelid.

The branches of the maple tree outside scratched at the windowpane. The radiator hissed. Anne had sat in that room hundreds of times. She had slept there. The room with its maple and its radiator and its water-stained ceiling was as familiar as her own, and yet the familiarity didn't comfort her.

She had been counting on Laura's house and on the chaos there that never changed. She had thought that in the Dewitts' kitchen, in Laura's room, she would feel as she had always felt there. She didn't. The familiarity itself disturbed her.

The room was like a blurred old photograph. Within its pale and curling edges were contained all the years of their childhood—hers and Laura's. There they had stood, little girls dressing up in their mothers' clothes. Anne shut her eyes, but beneath her lids the red Indian print skirt remained, troubling her memory.

It was because of Spencer. "I sometimes wonder what *you* remember." Well, forget Spencer, she told herself. What he said didn't matter.

"Your turn." Laura's voice came remotely through her thoughts. "Try whatever you want."

Anne stood up and walked to the bureau and fingered the sticks of eyeliner scattered there. "Would you mind if I didn't?"

"You don't want to?"

"I'm really not in the mood." It was too much like playing dress-up, too much like old times.

Laura nodded and took another look at herself in the mirror. "Don't you ever wear it?" she said. "Even for something special like tonight?"

"I never do."

"Oh," Laura said softly. "I would if I ever got the chance." She looked at Anne earnestly, eyes peering like a little girl's from under small purple lids.

"You'll have a chance."

"Maybe. Sometime." Then she said, "I want to show you something."

She began to dig her way into the closet she shared with Adele. Momentarily she disappeared, then from the depths of the closet she emerged with a dress on a hanger. It was a pretty shade of blue. "Isn't it beautiful?" she said. "I've never worn it."

"Is it yours?"

"Sure it's mine. I bought it with my birthday money."

She held the dress up against her on the hanger so that Anne could see the line.

"I bought it," Laura said, and then she hesitated. "Well, for a dumb reason. I bought it in case Benjamin might ask me to the fall dance at school. He didn't, of course. I mean, he was still here then, but he didn't."

She looked down at the dress that she held against her

body. "Anyway, now I have it." She smiled wryly at Anne. "Just in case, you know. So I don't mind."

But then, instead of shrugging and making a face as she would ordinarily have done, to Anne's horror Laura began to cry. She made no noise. She made no effort to hide the fact that she was crying. Tears squeezed out of the corners of her eyes and trailed slowly down her cheeks. Her face seemed to melt like a cake of soap left to soften in a soap dish. Anne said sharply, "Don't, Laura."

"Why not?" Laura stood there holding the dress and swaying a little. "Why shouldn't I? It's how I feel."

"Just don't. I'll get you a tissue."

Laura shook her head. She wiped her face with the back of her hand. "It's okay," she said. "Don't bother. I'm quitting."

Laura brushed again at the tears trailing sooty channels down her cheeks. She took a loud, shaking breath. "But I *do* mind, you know."

Anne swallowed. Something sharp-edged moved beneath her ribs. "You can't mind," she said unsteadily.

"I do."

"But you can't. That's the only way. You can't let yourself mind things. Just forget it."

Laura sniffed loudly and disappeared into the closet with the dress. When she reappeared, she looked at herself in the mirror and laughed. "I look like my eyes melted," she said, surveying the makeup, smeary on her cheeks. She spit on her fingers and began scrubbing at the streaks.

She had always been like that. Even as a little girl Laura

had been able to swing easily through feelings, changing them like trapezes in midair.

Anne sat, feeling the after flicker of pain beneath her ribs, and listened to the sound of Laura's voice. The flicker of pain, the troubled feelings faded. She was seeing the room through a telescope now or from a window many stories above. Laura said something, and Anne nodded but hardly heard.

Like a moat, Spencer had said, but that wasn't it. It was pure crystal she was looking through, a pane of glass.

The feeling stayed with her—walking home, having supper, changing her clothes. Before seven o'clock she was ready, standing at the living room window, waiting for Eric, and still the feeling remained, enclosing her like a transparent shell.

Snow had begun falling gently. She watched it feathering down past the streetlight—a swansdown snow, her mother would call it—and then she saw Eric appear at the end of the block, walking toward the house. Anne went to the door and opened it before he had time to ring the bell. She slipped out, pulling on a mitten, calling good-bye as the door closed.

There was a dusting of snow on his dark hair and on the shoulders of his jacket. He smiled at her uncertainly.

"Do you mind walking? I tried to get the car, but they wouldn't let me have it."

"No. I like walking in the snow."

"Different from the last time we walked down this street. Remember how hot it was?"

She remembered. Early September and the relentless scraping of the crickets.

"Right before you went to school."

Two days before.

He took her hand, and she let him. They turned the corner. He would ask her now about the letters she didn't write. Now or soon. But he didn't.

"We're going skiing between Christmas and New Year's," he said.

"Your family?"

"Even Sam. He's getting skis for Christmas."

She stopped and turned up the collar of her coat and felt snowflakes melting on her cheeks.

"In one way I'm looking forward to going," he said, "but in another way it seems too bad to be gone while you're home."

She looked at him around her collar. The point cut a little wedge from his cheek. She tried to remember how it had felt to be with him last summer, but the memory was like a snowflake melting on her sleeve, gone before she could describe it to herself.

"Anyway," he said, "we'll be back for New Year's Eve. I was wondering if you'd want to do something. Maybe there'll be a party."

"On New Year's Eve?" Anne said, and tried to think that far ahead.

"If you want to."

"I think so," she said, because the days seemed like a conveyor belt carrying her forward, and there seemed no point in saying either yes or no. She turned her face up to the snowflakes.

She knew most of the people in the bright living room. They said they were glad to see her. They asked if she missed University School. They asked about *her* school. Anne answered and let Eric take her coat upstairs and felt the strangeness of being there among them—felt, yet again, the sense of not sharing the same space and time.

In the dining room food was arranged in baskets and plates on the table. Anne took a pretzel and licked the salt. Stacy Hill came over to say hello. "Look at my hair," she said. "Frizz. From getting wet walking over here, damn it."

"It looks fine," Anne said. "Mine's probably strings."

"Did you and Eric walk?" Stacy said. "Hardly anyone could get cars." And that seemed strange, too, since before she'd left, hardly anyone was driving.

"Paul and I had a fight on the way over," Stacy said, "so he'll probably ignore me." She sighed an elaborately dramatic sigh. "Don't you wonder why they act the way they do? Just when you think some guy's going to be different, he turns out the same." She smoothed her hair. "They're clones."

Anne bit the pretzel. She couldn't think of what to say. "I'll bet somebody's got beer in his car," Stacy said. "I'll bet that's where he went."

"He'll probably be back in a minute."

Stacy shrugged. "Who cares?" She helped herself to a pretzel. "I mean *I* don't."

Martha Harmon came up, and she and Stacy began to talk about the vacation. Anne stood beside them and watched people moving around the table. Most of them she'd known since elementary school. Same faces, longer legs. She thought of Laura with the blue dress held against her, like a child crying grown-up tears.

"*Are* you, Anne?"

She turned.

"Are you going anywhere over vacation?"

She shook her head. "We never go away at Christmas."

Stacy began talking about her hair again. Anne finished her pretzel. By tomorrow Stacy would have forgotten her hair and her fight. Jill Norton, leaning against the table looking unhappy, would forget she had felt that way. By tomorrow the party would begin to fade and, in a few weeks when anyone remembered it, they would say it had been perfect. Whole pieces of what had once been real would vanish like snowflakes melting, Anne thought, leaving nothing but a memory of perfection.

She saw Eric appear in the doorway, looking for her. She had forgotten how tall he was, so tall that he stooped a little. She had forgotten the way he walked, crossing a room. "Would you like to dance?" he said. "They've got music in the basement."

There were candles in bottles and a standing lamp with its shade turned toward the wall and, in a few minutes, this was light enough to see by. Couples were moving slowly to the slow music, mysterious in the candlelight, like dancers on a dimly lit stage. Eric put his arm around her waist.

Anne watched the other couples across his shoulder and smelled wool and soap and warm laundry where her face touched his sweater. The record stopped. They waited while somebody changed it. Then they began to dance again.

She wasn't surprised when he kissed her. She had supposed he would. He kissed her while they were dancing, and when she said nothing, he kissed her again and they went on dancing.

They walked home in the still-falling snow. Eric talked about people, about skiing, and Anne watched the moon struggling around the ragged edge of a cloud.

"It isn't like it was last summer, is it?" he said all of a sudden.

Anne shook her head. "No."

"I guess it's because we haven't seen each other for a while."

Anne felt the cold flakes stinging her forehead. "No," she said, "it's because I'm different."

"You don't feel the same, do you?"

Anne took a deep breath. "I don't," she said. "I'm sorry."

He was quiet for a minute. "That's why you didn't write," he said. "That's what I thought, but I also hoped it might be different once you were home again."

Anne looked away at the struggling moon. She didn't want to see his face or know that he was hurt or think that he had cared enough to hope. There was nothing she could do. She couldn't help having no feelings left. And so again she said quietly, "I'm sorry."

"Why do you want to go out New Year's Eve then?" he said. "Just to be going?"

She couldn't blame him for sounding angry. She didn't know why she had said she'd go. It wasn't fair to him. "I shouldn't have said I'd go," she answered. "I don't know why I did."

There were two more blocks to walk, and they walked without speaking. Anne listened to the sound of passing cars filling the frozen space between them and remembered the sounds on summer nights as if they were someone else's memory.

At the door he said good night. There was nothing she could think to say except that she was sorry, and she'd said that twice before. She touched his shoulder with her mitten, quickly, gently, and went into the house.

The house was quiet. There was a lamp in the living room, left burning for her and for Spencer, whenever he came in. The door at the end of the upstairs hall was closed and there was no light beneath it.

Anne lay down on her bed. She pulled up the quilt and lay looking at the patch of moonlight—a frozen white lake on the floor of the bedroom.

Ten

She woke Sunday morning still dressed in the wrinkled clothes she had worn to the party. She turned stiffly on her side and felt the memory of the evening like a small cold stone beneath her ribs.

She could hear them downstairs getting breakfast, and after a while she changed her clothes and went down.

"How was it?" Spencer looked up from his eggs.

Anne found herself a plate and spooned scrambled eggs out of the frying pan. "It was fine."

"Good party?"

"I said fine."

The three of them had stopped eating and were looking at her expectantly. She was surrounded by questioning faces.

"Did you have a good time with Eric?"

"Spencer, I've told you that it was fine three times now. I saw a lot of people. We danced. Eric kissed me twice. We walked home."

"This isn't an inquisition," Spencer said.

"You asked."

Anne salted her eggs and reached for the pepper, and Dory began talking about something else.

Anne could feel Spencer looking at her. Even with her head bent she could feel his calm, thoughtful gaze leveled at her. He followed her upstairs after breakfast. She ignored him and began making the bed.

"You didn't have to say all that," he said.

"Why not?"

"Nobody was asking for details. That kissing business— that's private. You talked about it like—" Anne smoothed the blanket, waiting for whatever he was going to say. "Like—I don't know—like it made no difference."

"It didn't."

"But it's *supposed* to!"

Anne looked at him thoughtfully. "Listen, Spencer, if you think every time you kiss someone rockets go off, I've got news."

"You're quite an expert on the subject?"

She didn't answer him.

"Okay," he said, "maybe not rockets but *feelings*! Kissing someone isn't the equivalent of making a peanut butter sandwich, for God's sake."

Anne smoothed the spread and tucked it tightly over the

pillow. She moved slowly, gathering herself. "Quit it, Spencer," she said finally, very quietly. Then she turned and looked at him. "I want you to leave me alone. I really mean that. Ever since I got home you've been doing this. I want you to stop."

Spencer let out his breath loudly. "Stop worrying about you, you mean? Stop wondering what the hell's the matter with you?"

She said nothing, and after a while Spencer sighed. "Right," he said, tapping the doorjamb lightly with his fist, and then he was gone.

In the afternoon the sun came out and the eaves began to drip. Anne found her skates in the back hall closet and walked to the skating pond in the park behind her old elementary school. Mainly she went because she wanted to get away. Even alone in her room with the door closed she felt invaded by the presence of the rest of them.

The walk was so familiar it was almost automatic. She had walked to the pond for years, alone or with her mother, on days when the weather was so cold it made her head ache, or on others, like this one, when the sun and melting seemed borrowed from March.

She went into the warming shack to put on her skates. There were the usual number of kids with hockey sticks and knee pads, the few adults who skated for exercise. Small children in snowsuits lurched past on their ankles, faces like tomatoes fringed with snow. The wood stove crackled. The shack smelled of singed mittens.

Anne laced up her skates and walked out the door and

onto the ice. She glided once around the pond easily. She was a strong skater. There had even been a time when she was a serious skater, practicing figures several times a week with her mother.

She circled the pond again, dodging children staggering on the ice. She remembered doing that, looking down to see her own ankles turned over like Raggedy Ann feet in new white skates, wondering if she would ever stand firmly on the blades. She glided past the children and on around the pond.

Ahead there was a patch of ice momentarily deserted. She skated into a figure eight, leaning on her outside edge. The figure was fair. A little jerky, but not bad for the first time in several years. She skated through the figure again and then once more, growing serious. She'd always had trouble with the second loop. It had never been smooth enough. She started into the figure again, listening to the sound of her blade cutting ice, feeling her way into the long glide and again, at the second turn, faltering.

She felt her old sense of frustration at never being able to get it right. She could hear her mother's voice saying, "All right now, get control of yourself and try again." She could almost see her mother sweeping smoothly through the figure to show her how it ought to be done, in perfect control, calmly. Her mother was able to do it without a ghost of uncertainty.

Then Anne would try—ten, twelve, fifteen times— never getting it smooth enough. With each attempt she would feel her body growing more rigid, her legs tighter and, so, more awkward.

"If you let yourself get upset, you'll never do it proper-ly." She wasn't sure if she'd said it aloud or had only heard the voice of memory. But she knew it was true. To lose control was the worst thing you could do. It was courting disaster.

She skated through the figure again. Then she began to skate it repeatedly. Gradually the turn began to smooth out. It wasn't perfect, but it was better. She went into it smoothly and felt the turn gather and run out along the blade as if her body had become a part of it, an extension of the steel. Ice on ice, coolly cutting a shape. And then the jerk. Teeth clenched, she started again, trying to feel nothing but the movement of the turn.

The sun had dropped below the trees when, at last, she was too tired to try it again. That meant nothing in December. It might be no later than four o'clock, but she was tired and she was cold. In the warmth of the shack, she took off her skates and looped them together over her shoulder. She shivered, going outside into the fading afternoon.

The puddles on the sidewalk were beginning to skin over. A child passed her, pulling a sled. He was dragging it by a rope along the bare sidewalk, and the sound of the runners on the concrete made Anne shudder. "Why don't you pull that damned thing on the snow?" she shouted after him. The child stopped and looked at her. He was only a little kid in a red nylon snowsuit. Instantly she was sorry.

She and Spencer washed the dinner dishes. Later she tried to work on the paper, but the child with the sled and the angry words that had erupted before she could stop them troubled her. It was hard to think. She heard Spencer go out. She heard Dory come upstairs. She closed the notebook and decided to get a glass of milk and then go to bed.

There was a strip of light under the kitchen door. Her father was reading at the table and having his nightly bowl of cornflakes. He slid his glasses down his nose. "Still up?"

"It's only ten."

She took a glass from the dishwasher and poured herself some milk.

"Keep me company?" He was wearing an old beige sweater that her mother had patched with leather on the elbows. Anne carried her glass to the table and sat down.

"Is everything going all right for you, Annie?" he said, surprising her.

"Why do you ask that?"

"Fatherly curiosity," he said. "Concern."

"I suppose Spencer has been complaining."

"Nope. I've just been wondering whether you had something on your mind."

She sipped her milk and looked past him at the rack above the sink where a towel hung askew. "Nothing special."

"I see that you covered the roses," he said.

"Somebody had to."

"It would have pleased your mother."

Anne nodded briefly. "That's why I did it."

He looked at her thoughtfully, spoon in midair, reminding her of Spencer eating soup. "You were always good about that," he said.

"Mother would have done a better job."

He gazed at his spoon and frowned. "Your mother was good at a great many things," he said, and Anne nodded. "I think things came easily to her in the first place. Sometimes it was difficult for her to understand that for other people they came harder."

There was a tone in his voice that she couldn't have described. It was there and then it was gone, but the sound brushed like wings at the back of her mind. "Are you through with your cornflakes?" she said.

"Not quite," he said. "I'm poky."

She sipped her milk and sat waiting, just as she had waited for Spencer in the restaurant. They never hurried, either of them. "The twentieth century will pass them right by while they watch the grass grow," her mother had sometimes said.

Then he looked up at her with Spencer's mild, blinking gaze. "Is it all right being home?" he asked almost shyly. "Are you getting along with Dory?"

"No problem."

"I hope not. I really want the two of you to be happy." He stopped eating entirely then and leaned back in the chair. "Both you and Dory mean a great deal to me," he said. He seemed to be speaking more to himself than to her. Anne moved restlessly, tracing a figure on the table top, concentrating on that rather than on the sound of his voice.

Eventually he began to eat again, clicking his spoon against the bottom of the bowl. At last he finished. Anne stood up and took her glass and his bowl to the sink. She rinsed them, turned, and looked at the patches sewn firmly on his sleeves. Then she turned on the water and rinsed out the sink.

"You going to bed?"

She said that she was and started toward the door. Midway she stopped and turned around. "Did we ever go away at Christmastime?" she asked.

"What makes you think of that now?"

"People were talking about going away over vacation at the party the other night. I said we never did."

"Almost never," he replied, and she thought he was going to say something else, but before he had begun to say it, she had started upstairs.

Later she heard him come up. Later still, she heard Spencer. She was awake because she was thinking that "almost" meant not quite never. "Almost" could mean sometimes or once.

On Monday, in the dentist's waiting room, Anne sat on a straight-backed chair and looked through a copy of *Scientific American*. It was that kind of waiting room—straight chairs, *Scientific American*, and a half dozen pamphlets on brushing teeth. She was looking at the new photographs of Saturn, which, even shown close-up and in detail, was dependably still the ringed planet of sixth-grade astronomy.

To her, the stars in the sky had always been just as she had observed them on the sixth-grade star chart—fixed and unmoving, although she knew that they rose and sank and changed.

Dr. O'Brien's hygienist called her to come in and settled her with a bib in the reclining chair. Like the office, the hygienist was serious. She worked away at Anne's teeth in silence. Anne looked at the acoustical tile on the ceiling and imagined galaxies.

Finally the hygienist put her tools aside and splashed Anne's mouth with a stream of warm water. "We'll give you your next appointment for June," she said. "You'll be home in June, right?"

Anne grunted, meaning neither yes nor no. June seemed much farther away than Saturn. But the hygienist took the grunt for a yes and gave her a pink appointment card.

"Hard to imagine June in this weather, isn't it?" she said. Now, with the job done, she was chatty. She wondered what Anne wanted for Christmas. Clothes, Anne said, because that answer was easiest. But she realized she had not thought about that any more than she had thought about June.

Rounding the corner outside the dentist's office, she saw Dory coming out of Kresge's with an armload of packages. Dory stopped outside the door, disheveled in her plaid wool coat, and began rearranging them. Then she looked up and saw Anne.

"Do you want some help carrying those?" Anne said.

"Are you going home? That would be wonderful."

Outside the lighted plate-glass windows of the store they transferred half the packages to Anne's arms while shoppers dodged around them.

"I'm such a fool," Dory said. "I went in there for shelf paper and look at me."

"What did you buy?"

"Tree ornaments. I couldn't restrain myself. They had the cutest things. When we get home I'll show you."

Anne could imagine them, like the dyed carnations in the Chinese vase. "Have you ever looked at all the boxes of ornaments in the attic?" she asked.

"You know I've never been up there." Dory chuckled. "Attics just mean cleaning to me. My mother used to say her attic was so bad she was just going to wall it off."

Anne looked up at the Kresge sign. "Ours isn't like that."

They started up State Street together, Anne trying to shorten her steps to suit Dory's. She felt gigantic walking beside her. Her feet, her hands, her legs—everything was twice the size of Dory's. She hunched her shoulders around the packages and half listened to the story that Dory was telling her.

It surprised her that Dory had never been in the attic. She hadn't thought that there was any place in the house that was still untouched. She could imagine the cartons of Christmas ornaments, stacked against the attic wall, containing the tiny painted lambs from Austria, the crystal stars, the bright tin fish, the pastel angels with pale silk wings that, year after year, they had hung on the tree.

Christmas Eve. The tree shining softly in the dim and fragrant living room, the angels and stars and lambs in place and her mother at the piano. They had sung carols on Christmas Eve. Her mother led them with her strong, clear voice, and Anne sat curled beside her father in his chair, singing, with her cheek against his sweater.

She remembered the bowl of nuts and purple raisins on the table, firelight and music and port in a cut-glass decanter, catching the light of the fire, the light of the tree, shining like a deep brown ruby within a crystal star.

Anne closed her eyes, swept with memory, and Dory said, "The car's on the fritz."

"Broken?"

"You should have heard your father when it wouldn't start this morning, poor man. He really hates that car."

"No, he doesn't," Anne said sharply. "He and my mother chose that car together." But even as she said it, she knew Dory was right. Her father had never liked the car. It had been her mother's choice.

"Maybe he was just mad at the starter," Dory said.

But it wasn't that. He had never wanted it. Her mother drove it when they went out. Anne looked up at the twilight sky. Maybe there were other things like the car. The rosebushes? The pier glass table that he always bumped with the closet door? The eucalyptus leaves? The Christmas trees? Anne felt doubt move like shifting sand. She redoubled her efforts to match her steps to Dory's.

He had chosen Dory, after all. So different. So small. So

unlike Anne's mother and Anne herself. But he had chosen her. Anne looked down at the sidewalk. The concrete no longer seemed firm beneath her boots.

She had walked this street a million times as a child at twilight, hurrying home toward light and warmth and order. Or was that true? Were the nights, the days, the Christmases as she remembered, or was there another way of remembering them? Had whole pieces of what had once been real vanished like snowflakes melting? Was this what Spencer was telling her?

Cars went past them on the hill, making flattened sounds in the cold. Dory chattered, but Anne didn't listen. She looked at the houses they were passing, lighted windows where curtains had not yet been pulled against the dark. She concentrated on the lights, pushing against an uncertainty that made them swim before her eyes, wheeling unsteadily as stars.

Eleven

"Over the river and through the woods to grand-mother's house we go—" The song occupied Anne's mind like an uninvited guest.

She walked, unwillingly in time to its cadence, on her way to choir rehearsal on Tuesday. Two beats to a square of sidewalk, all the way to the church. She pulled open the old oak doors with a kind of relief, as if she had reached a place where the song couldn't follow, and went in.

The church was cold and smelled of beeswax candles. In the dim reaches of the choir stalls there was the buzz and rattle of the choir assembling, the tentative sounds of the accompanist playing chords. Anne started to take off her coat, changed her mind, and started down the side aisle. There was never any heat in the church for rehearsals—an economy that made her associate rehearsals with numb fingertips.

Laura had saved her a place in the alto section. "I didn't get a bit of sleep last night," she said immediately, and, looking at her, Anne thought it might be true. "All night I was worrying about my damned English paper."

"When is it due?" Anne unwound her scarf.

"Thursday. Last day of school. Just to make sure we don't start enjoying ourselves early."

Anne sat down next to her on the bench. "Haven't you started it yet?" She was suddenly sure that Laura had not.

"I haven't even picked a poem to write about!" Laura's face was a study in misery.

"Do you have a list of poems?"

"Oh, sure. But you know me and poetry. The trouble with poems, they're all words."

"Just pick a short one," Anne said.

Hope stirred briefly in Laura's eyes. "Maybe a short one—"

"I bet Browning's on the list, for instance. He's not too hard."

"For you maybe. For you nothing's hard."

Which wasn't true, of course. Dante had been hard. So was Conrad.

But not Browning. She had known poems by Browning since she was a little girl.

> The year's at the spring
> And day's at the morn;

> Morning's at seven;
> The hillsides dew-pearled—

The lark's on the wing; and then something about a snail. Anne frowned. The snail's on the thorn: Oh, and then,

> God's in his heaven—
> All's right with the world.

Anne looked across the nave to where Mr. Babbitt was speaking to the pianist, but she saw the open windows in the dining room and sunlight lying like honey on her toast and heard her mother saying those lines from Browning because it was the first real morning of spring.

She turned to Laura, who was staring gloomily at the music in her hands. "We can talk about it after rehearsal if you want."

Laura's round face lit up. "Could we?" she said. "That'd really help."

Mr. Babbitt came over and said hello to Anne. Other people, straggling into place, said hello. For a moment she was a stranger being greeted, and then it was exactly as it had always been. She discovered that she remembered her parts in most of the carols, and, for an hour, singing, sharing the music with Laura, she felt it might have been any December of her life.

Laura was eager to get going when the rehearsal was over. For once she moved quickly and was ready—coat, scarf, and ragged mittens—before most of the choir had gathered up the music. "Where shall we go?" Laura said. "If we go to my house, we'll probably have to sit in the furnace room so as not to disturb the great minds at work."

"You can come to mine. Nobody will be home yet."

"How great," Laura said wistfully.

"Beauty's in the eye of the beholder."

"What do you mean?"

Anne pushed open the church doors. "I mean it depends on who you are, how you look at things."

"Everyone in your family talks like a book," Laura said.

"We read them."

"I think it's because of your mother. I remember she talked just like a poem," Laura said, and looked worried. "No offense."

"Laura, you don't have to apologize for mentioning my mother."

"I know I don't. Except I worry that I'll make you feel bad."

"Well, don't."

They cut across the parking lot outside the church and started their usual zigzag path home. "Most people have such rotten mothers," Laura said. "Look at mine. All she does is sit up in the attic writing her dissertation. Once in a while she comes down and tries to get on my nerves."

"Mine wasn't that way."

"That's what I mean. You never said a bad word about her."

"There was never anything bad to say."

They turned into the Lincoln Street alley, passed trash cans and the shabby backs of garages, indistinct in the windy twilight. Anne let them into the yard through the alley gate, and Laura followed her to the house.

They sat on the floor in the living room. Laura produced a crumpled list of poems stuffed between the pages of her English book. "Any of these," she said. "I don't care."

Anne read over the list. "There *is* one of Browning's," she said. " 'My Last Duchess.' I've read that."

"Corning mentioned it in class. It's a dramatic something or other."

"Monologue. Let me just read it over."

When she had finished, she handed the book to Laura. "You read it now. That way we can discuss it. It won't be like I'm telling you."

She watched Laura frowning over the words and tried to imagine how it would feel to have such difficulty with a poem.

"I kind of remember this," Laura said, looking up.

"Well, what do you think it's about?"

"This guy—this Duke—who's talking."

"All right, but what's he talking about? That's what you need to know."

"I *know* that's what I *need* to know. But I don't."

Anne got up and switched on another lamp. "Try."

"He's talking about his wife who died. Only—I don't know—it seems like it's not really *about* her."

Anne sat down again. "Of course it is." It was no

wonder Laura had trouble, she thought. "Look, it begins,

> "That's my last Duchess painted on the wall,
> Looking as if she were alive.

What does that tell you?"

"He's looking at a painting."

"All right. Go on."

"I can't."

"It's a picture of the Duke's wife, okay? And she's dead. What you need to look at is how he feels about her."

Laura nodded.

"So what do you know? He's lonely, right? That's why he keeps talking about her. He's going to marry some Count's daughter—you get that in the last lines—but that is irrelevant to him. Mostly the poem is about how he misses his first wife."

Laura looked confused. "I don't see it," she said. "It doesn't seem to me that he cares much about anyone."

Anne sighed. "How can you miss seeing it?"

"Mrs. Corning said—" Laura looked up hopefully. "I remember she said he was self-centered."

Anne stretched in exasperation. "He's mourning, Laura! Can't you see that? He feels terrible. I don't care what Mrs. Corning said."

"Well, if he feels so terrible, how come he's getting married again?"

There was a pause, a kind of momentary vacuum in the room. Anne got to her feet. "I don't know," she said. And then, because she wanted to move, "I'm going upstairs. I'll be back in a minute."

She went into her room to get a sweater, and while she was there she heard the side door slam. When she came back down, Spencer was in the living room unzipping his jacket.

"Spencer says he *is* self-centered," Laura said almost apologetically.

"Sure he is. The guy's an egomaniac." Spencer dumped his coat on the sofa. "He's not interested in anyone but himself."

Anne sat down on the arm of the sofa and looked unbelievingly at the two of them. Laura she could understand, but Spencer surely knew more about poetry than that. "How can you possibly say that?" she asked Spencer.

"It's true. That's how."

"If two of us think so—" Laura began.

"Everyone thinks so," Spencer said flatly, and started upstairs.

"I don't," Anne said. "I don't think that at all."

Spencer turned on the stairs and blinked at her mildly. "I suppose there always has to be a minority opinion," he said.

On Thursday morning the sun shone. The backyard was filled with a twittering of sparrows. Anne stood at the kitchen window watching them flutter and settle on the spilled seed around the feeder and knew that she was procrastinating.

In the week she had been home she had made essentially no progress on the paper she had thought she could write so easily. Maybe Mrs. Liggett was right—the book was too hard. Maybe—and yet, almost at once, something in her rejected the idea that she couldn't do it. As her mother had told her often enough, doing anything was mainly a matter of working hard.

And she did have one good sentence. It had come to her like a present a few days before. She had copied it down with the feeling of certainty that comes with a good idea. It seemed to touch the heart of the matter. Anne smiled wryly to herself. The heart of *Heart of Darkness*, she thought, and steeled herself to get at it.

She stood a minute in the doorway to her room, admiring its orderliness. It was the only room in the house that had remained in the state of order that had once been the rule everywhere. Her bed was smoothly made. The books on the desk were neatly stacked.

Anne put on a pair of woolen socks and sat down at the desk with determination. It was a matter of thinking hard, of concentrating. That was all. She had learned to do that long ago—memorizing a piano piece, learning multiplication tables. She leaned her cheek on her hand and began to concentrate on Conrad.

She looked at her notebook for the sentence that had seemed so promising. The words sat tidily on the page as she had written them, but she was no longer so certain she understood. "Conrad's main character, Marlow, takes a journey to the heart of darkness, which is both a voyage up the Congo into Africa and a journey into the darkness within himself."

Anne frowned. It was like looking at a sentence someone else had written. What had she meant by "both"? What did "the darkness within himself" mean? She ran a hand through her hair. The sense that the words had come like a present began to desert her.

She sat tapping her pencil on the notebook's metal edge. She had to understand. Or she had to scratch the sentence and begin again. Either way she had to get on with it. She needed an A on the paper to do all right for the semester. There had been the trouble about the midterm. Anne shook herself involuntarily at the thought of the midterm. She had to understand this book.

Marlow was afraid of the darkness. But why? What was so threatening, after all, if you had guns and men and a boat whistle that terrified attackers? And Marlow had all those. It was something else.

She looked at the sentence she had written, and it seemed as unfamiliar now as if she had never seen it before. Marlow was afraid of the wilderness outside and the darkness within, and somehow those two were the same. Conrad meant one to stand for the other.

She got up and wandered out of the room, down the hall as far as Spencer's door and back again. She stood at her window, looking at the sparrows, staring like a passenger on a train, she thought, looking for signs of the next town or crossing.

Oddly, the minute she thought of a train she could see a whole scene clearly. She knew the stale smell the train would have and how the overhead lights glared on the faces of the other passengers. Absently she wandered back to the desk and opened the notebook to a fresh page. Almost dreamily, she began to write about the train.

There were men folding coats and tucking them onto the overhead racks. There was a Milky Way wrapper crushed in the aisle. There was a woman in a knitted hat—a purple knitted hat—reading a paperback Ross Macdonald. Anne felt curiously certain of both the color and the title. Across the aisle from the woman a child sat holding a stuffed blue rabbit. Her feet dangled, not quite touching the floor.

Anne leaned on her elbow. Her hair made a curtain around her face. Gradually, as often happened when she wrote, the room receded and time moved without her noticing. She discovered the train's slick plastic seats, the sudden burst of noise at the end of the car when the door opened. The scene seemed clear to her in its smallest detail.

Only gradually did she become aware that the clock downstairs was striking noon and that she had spent the morning doing nothing but writing about a train.

She stood up, thoroughly impatient with herself. She had promised to meet Laura at noon for lunch to celebrate the last half-day of school and now she was late. Conrad's novel lay like an accusation on the desk, half-buried in a wilderness of notebook paper.

The Dewitts' kitchen smelled of dogs. When Anne arrived, Laura was already making peanut butter sandwiches. She was jubilant. "No more school until January," she said. "If you say it like that it seems longer." She waved the peanut butter-covered knife like a baton. "I handed in the paper. It stunk, but so what? It's over."

"Did you do the Browning poem?"

"No, I got too confused. I finally wrote on this sonnet of Shakespeare's."

Overhead Mrs. Dewitt's typewriter rattled, flurries of clicking followed by long silences. Laura looked at the ceiling. "Maybe she'll win the Nobel prize," she said. "Better her than me."

Anne watched Laura scraping the bottom of the jar, rattling the knife against the jar's glass side. One of the dogs yawned enormously. "Did I tell you Gwendolyn had puppies?" Laura said. "She had them in the closet Saturday night. Want to see them?"

She brought two of the puppies into the kitchen and put them on the table beside the peanut butter jar. They sprawled blindly, searching the air with their noses.

"All they do so far is eat," said Laura.

Anne stroked the smaller of the two with a finger. It struggled up awkwardly as if trying to stand, then sprawled flat again. "Poor thing," Anne said.

Laura grinned. "It's like me and my paper."

Gwendolyn stood anxiously beside the table, neck craning to see the puppies.

"She wants him to stand up," Anne said.

"No. He's too little."

"But she wants him to."

Laura slapped tops onto the sandwiches. "You're seeing

things," she said. "Take them off the table, will you, so I can pour the milk."

Anne took the puppies into her lap and held them while Laura got a milk carton out of the refrigerator. Gwendolyn stood beside Anne, leaning on her leg. "She never takes her eyes off them," Anne said.

"Put them on the floor and watch her."

As soon as the puppies were on the floor Gwendolyn nuzzled each one all over, pushing at it with her nose. "You see?" Anne said. "She's trying to teach them. She wants them to stand."

"You're nuts." Laura put each sandwich on a plate and cut it in half. "Want some stale potato chips?" she said.

Anne shook her head, intent on the puppies. They skidded and floundered on the slippery linoleum and Gwendolyn nudged them with her nose. "They're trying so hard," she said.

"What else have they got to do? Personally, I don't think it would be a bad life if all you had to do was eat and slide around on the floor."

"They look like little children on skates," Anne said, and they did, slipping and sprawling pathetically on the slippery floor.

She was watching the puppies so intently that when Mrs. Dewitt came into the kitchen, at first she didn't hear her. "I thought I heard voices down here," Mrs. Dewitt said. "Hi, Anne."

Anne looked up vaguely, still engrossed in the puppies' struggles, and smiled. She liked Mrs. Dewitt.

Mrs. Dewitt wasn't a pretty woman, although she might have been if she'd cared. Her hair straggled from an uncertain knot on the back of her head, and she was wearing the baggy pants and furry slippers that were very nearly her uniform. She turned on the gas under the teakettle. "How's school, Anne?"

Laura groaned. "Do we have to talk about school?" she said. "Anybody's?"

Mrs. Dewitt put a tea bag into a cup. "Why don't you put those puppies back, Laura? Poor old Gwendolyn looks like she could use some peace and quiet."

"Nobody's bothering her."

"I think she feels better when they're all in one place."

Anne looked down at the sprawling puppies, soft baby lumps on the smooth floor.

"Really, I mean it, Laura. Put them back before Gwendolyn gets cross."

"She's fine."

"Please," Mrs. Dewitt said loudly, "just *do* it!"

Laura looked up at her mother. Anne had seen that stubborn expression on Laura's face many times. "There's nothing wrong with Gwendolyn," Laura said. "She doesn't mind having her puppies around. She's not writing any damned dissertation."

Anne glanced up apprehensively. Mrs. Dewitt's back was turned. For a minute she said nothing.

Then suddenly, inexplicably, Mrs. Dewitt burst out laughing. "I hear you," she said, and kept laughing, and Anne looked from Laura to her mother in bewilderment.

"Laura's got a point," Mrs. Dewitt said to Anne. "The whole family is suffering with this dissertation of mine."

"You can say that again," Laura muttered. Then she picked up the puppies and carried them back to the closet.

That was all there was to it. Mrs. Dewitt finished making her tea and went back upstairs. Anne and Laura finished their sandwiches. Gwendolyn yawned and fell asleep. By the time they left for rehearsal, Laura's spirits were fully restored. Anne realized that only she had taken the incident seriously. What had she thought would happen, after all? Laura and her mother argued all the time.

The rehearsal ran late. Mr. Babbitt was dissatisfied with the way they sounded, and he kept them an extra quarter of an hour, going over one of the new carols.

"You can't satisfy him," Laura said. "If a bunch of angels came flying into church singing their heads off, he'd say they were flat."

Anne looked up at the darkening sky—a translucent snow sky—and imagined angels. "He just wants it to be good," she said.

"No. He wants it to be perfect."

"So?"

"So that's unrealistic, given us."

"Not really. If we worked harder we'd be a lot closer to perfect anyway. That's what he had in mind."

Laura appeared unconvinced. "See you tomorrow," she said, and they parted at the usual corner.

Walking home, Anne felt hypocritical to have spoken of working hard. Wasn't that just what she hadn't been doing? For the second or third time that day she promised herself that she wouldn't waste any more time.

The house sailed up ahead of her like a ghost ship in the snowlight. Once in the side door, she hurried to turn on lights.

In the sudden harsh brightness of the kitchen, she saw the remains of lunch—the usual accumulation of dishes on the drainboard, a wrinkled bread wrapper on the counter. On the table were coffee cups and a pile of papers her father had apparently been reading. It seemed strange to her that he had chosen to work there, oblivious of the mess. Beneath the table a pair of Dory's shoes lay collapsed like weary birds. On the oven door there was a smear of grape jam. It could as well have been the Dewitts' kitchen, Anne thought, but she made no move to clean up.

Instead, she sat down in her father's chair and listened to the furnace grumbling softly in the cellar. The house had a hundred voices if you listened, she thought, an invisible ghost life of sounds. Every doorknob, every saucer contained the reflected images of everyone who had used them. The floors held ghostly footsteps. At that moment she was being gathered into the kitchen's memory, becoming part of the story that the house told when it sighed and cracked in the dark.

She stood up and wandered into the living room. A day-old newspaper was strewn on the sofa. Beyond the sofa was the piano, open as if someone had just stopped playing. It shone in the lamplight.

Anne touched the cracked keys gently—cracked because

they were really ivory and very old. Hesitantly she played a chord and listened to it echo and fade, joining the ghost sounds in the empty room.

She hadn't wanted to touch the piano much since her mother died. But now she sat down on the bench and played another chord, then another, without taking her eyes off the music rack where her old blue music book had stood, and in it the circle of key signs her mother had drawn for her. She could see the book in her mind's eye, and the circle, neatly drawn.

She closed her eyes and struck more notes. The piano was terribly out of tune. Nobody would bother to have it tuned now, she supposed, but once Mr. Beach had come to the house every couple of months to make sure it was perfect. She could remember his staccato tapping and the eerie glide a note made as he tightened a tuning pin. And later, she remembered, her mother would play to test it—shimmering runs up and down the keyboard—to make sure Mr. Beach had done a good job.

Idly, she listened to her fingers roving the keys. So many of the ghost sounds in the house would be melodies. She imagined her mother's bright, invisible melodies clustering in the air around her and, someplace among them, the music her own clumsy fingers had made, practicing after school.

After school and every afternoon in the summer. She saw the summer sunlight in the living room making the patterns in the rug glow like stained glass, the wood of the piano shine like satin. She could almost hear the whispering sprinkler outside the open windows, and her mother's voice, counting. "You have to learn to count it, darling, if you want to play it in time."

And so, counting. Squinting at the red book her mother had found that contained simplified versions of music she herself played. For an hour every afternoon, squinting and counting.

After the hour she could sit on the rug's melting colors and listen to her mother play. Cascades of ivory and silver notes spilled onto the rug around her like brilliant rain. "That's how you will play someday, Anne." She had understood, sitting among rich colors, silver and ivory, that that was how she would play someday if she worked hard.

Anne touched the keys again. Her fingers hunted over them, searching a tune. They seemed to move by themselves. They played a measure and then another while she sat, bewildered to hear a melody she hadn't known she still remembered filling the room—one of the simple ones from the old red book—"Humoresque."

Then, as quickly as she had begun to play, she stopped. The notes died in mid-measure and she couldn't go on. She stood up and closed the lid over the keyboard and went to the window to see if the snow had begun.

She had never been able to play beyond the point where her fingers stopped. She had never learned the whole thing. But she couldn't think why.

Abruptly she turned from the window. She heard a key in the side door and Spencer stamping his feet in the hall.

After dinner Anne scraped plates and settled them one by one in the dishwasher. It had been nearly full when she started, and she had to search for a slot to hold the last plate. She held it in one hand, irritably rearranging the contents of the machine, and then, unaccountably, she dropped it. One moment it was in her fingers, the next it lay broken on the floor.

Pieces of its deep blue border scattered across the linoleum. Anne stared at the shards with the half-frightened feeling that any broken thing always gave her. Clearly it was beyond repair. She found the dustpan and a broom and began to sweep up the pieces.

They lay scattered as if the plate had exploded. One of her mother's favorite plates. Favorite, Anne thought, because of the border—the deep blue that was her mother's color. Then, drawing in her breath, Anne swept up the scraps.

The door from the dining room swung open and Dory came in. "I broke a plate," Anne said. "One of the good ones."

Dory bent to hold the dustpan. "That makes two," she said. "I dropped one the other day." Then she stopped and looked curiously at Anne's face. "It's all right," she said gently. "They're only plates."

"But they're the good ones. I should have been more careful."

"You didn't mean to drop it."

Anne shook her head, looking at the collection of scraps in the dustpan, white and blue the color of hyacinths.

"My mother always said, 'We can replace broken dishes,'" Dory added. "It was bones she worried about."

"Bones?"

"You know—legs, arms." Dory shook the dustpan into the wastebasket. "Compared to those, plates are easy."

And for just that minute it did seem easy, seemed exactly as Dory said—just a plate.

Twelve

Snow began to fall in the night. Anne woke and heard its soft hushing against the house. She slept again and dreamed of snow, falling steadily past the windows of a train.

In the morning the yard lay deeply blanketed. Drifts hemmed the car into the open garage. But by ten o'clock the sun wavered across the windowsill into the study, where Anne was sitting at her father's desk.

It had been a magical act, carrying her notebook down to the study, as if changing desks would change her power to concentrate. But, sitting there, she was aware of the sun, aware of the mailtruck spinning its wheels in the driveway, aware that a dog was barking someplace beyond the

Mortimers' hedge. The single sentence she had counted on lay, isolated and spiritless, on the notebook page, and she began to wonder whether she had ever really understood it at all.

She understood that she needed an A. That fact was clear. It was possibly the only thing that still seemed clear to her. She picked up her father's letter opener and studied it for clues. On one side of the desk, notes for the book he was always trying to finish were bound haphazardly together in a pile of worn binders. On the other was a copper bowl her mother had always kept filled with fresh flowers.

Anne felt certain that the words she needed were hovering somewhere just out of reach and that if she could capture one or two, the others would somehow follow. She sat looking at the letter opener, turning its steel blade to catch the light. She had to have an A, she thought, and then, abruptly, she wondered why.

The question took her by surprise. For a minute it gave her a lovely whirling sensation of freedom. For a minute it seemed to her that she was spinning at the edge of limitless possibility, beyond expectation and demand. But the next minute the spinning ceased and she knew why she needed to have an A. Because of the midterm, that business.

She didn't understand what had happened during the midterm. She had taken plenty of tests before. She had read the questions, and they were easy. But *something* had happened. She was required to choose three—that was how it had begun, with the choosing.

She remembered that the room was hot. She remembered steam hissing in the radiators. She looked at the sheet of mimeographed questions, glanced at her roommate five seats away, who had already chosen and begun to write, and looked back at the questions. The purple mimeographed letters bewildered her. She turned toward the window, looking at the cloudy November sky.

The bare trees beyond the hockey field reminded her of grade school art, stick drawings of trees scratching a crayoned sky. And the dog stopping to sniff them seemed crayoned, too.

When she turned back to the questions, ten minutes of the hour had already passed.

She tried to concentrate. The questions concerned poems, all of which they'd read in class. Besides that, she'd studied them well. After more minutes she chose some lines by Emily Dickinson and settled herself down to write.

After great pain, a formal feeling comes. Mrs. Liggett had said the poem was an image of mourning. She said that it spoke of the stages that a person passed through in the process.

Anne remembered that much, gazing at the sheet of questions, but she couldn't think how to begin. The radiators sighed. Behind her someone rattled paper. Her thoughts jumbled, and she sat holding her pen above the paper as if she were paralyzed. Beyond the window the crayon dog still circled the trees.

"The poem gives us three images," she wrote. "The first—" She scratched out those words and looked at the clock. "Of the three, the first—" "The first of the three—" "Emily Dickinson gives us three—"

"Thirty minutes," Mrs. Liggett said, and Anne heard the words as if they were meant for her personally. "The first image that appears—" She *knew* the poem. She understood it just as she understood that the trees outside the window were three-dimensional, and yet she couldn't write.

> After great pain, a formal feeling comes—
> The Nerves sit ceremonious, like Tombs—
> The stiff Heart questions . . .

Anne reread the lines and looked at the clock and knew that she had to begin again, had to write something.

"Of the three images—" She bent over the paper. Her sentences limped awkwardly, graceless as sticks. She wrote as if she had just learned to write sentences.

"Of the three, the first—" Before she had finished a paragraph, a few girls were beginning to hand in papers. With a feeling of desperation, she thought that perhaps she didn't understand the poem at all, but it was too late now to start over.

With barely fifteen minutes left, Anne gripped the pencil and forced sentence after wooden sentence onto the page, writing—badly, she knew—about something she didn't understand. The radiators whispered, "But you know that you can do better than that." She tried not to hear them, tried to work faster. With rising anxiety she wrote, gripping the pencil so hard her fingers ached.

Deep in the building the furnace groaned. Pens scratched. Paper rustled. "Ten minutes."

Anne leaned on her fist, writing furiously now in a hand she scarcely recognized—big and loose and messy as a child's—while the radiators whispered, "But you know you can do better." She wrote faster, covering the page with scrawl, writing words that meant nothing to her, while the hissing radiators whispered in her ears.

Mrs. Liggett called for the papers. Anne looked up frantically. She had never in her life not finished an exam. Mrs. Liggett came down the aisle, collecting papers. "Anne, you'll have to stop now," she said when she reached her desk.

"I'm not finished."

"Then you'll have to hand in what you've done."

"But it's no good and I'm not through and—" And suddenly, as though a hand had clapped over her mouth, she was silent. She handed the exam to Mrs. Liggett, picked up her books, and, saying nothing else, walked out of the room.

In the hall girls were comparing notes. Anne went past them into an empty classroom. She stood at the window looking out over the empty hockey field. She might fail. If she was lucky, she'd get a D.

What had happened? She pressed her forehead against the cold pane. "When you've done the best you can, then you should try to do better." She *had* tried.

She leaned against the window frame. The dog was no longer wandering among the trees at the edge of the field.

The sun had appeared, looking not at all like a sea urchin as her mother used to point out, although Anne remembered that she'd drawn it looking that way for years. Someplace at the back of her closet, Anne thought, there was still a shoebox full of pictures of spiky yellow suns. She put down the letter opener and looked at her notebook. The sentence lay like a remonstrance on the page.

Well, there were other books if she couldn't understand this one. There was a whole list to choose from. The study shelves were full of novels, and there were others in her mother's bookcase in the bedroom. Probably any book on Mrs. Liggett's list could be found somewhere in the house if she looked.

The clock in the kitchen whirred and struck. Anne stood up, intending to search the study shelves, but found, instead, that she was climbing the stairs. Surely it would be all right to go into their room to find a book.

Bare feet silent on the soft rose rug, she crossed the room and knelt beside her mother's bookcase. The worn spines under her fingertips were like acquaintances met after a long absence. Jane Austen, Trollope, *Middlemarch*, volumes of poetry arranged by author. Hitching on the balls of her feet, she moved along the lowest shelf, looking at her mother's favorite books until she came to one, odd among the others. It was her own copy of *The Secret Garden*. They had put it there to honor it because it was her own favorite.

She stroked its old spotted binding affectionately. She had read it a dozen times, summer after summer afternoon on her grandmother's porch in Wisconsin, while the lake lapped quietly against the shore below and the breeze rustled in the leaves of the pin oaks.

Spencer fished those afternoons, her grandmother napped, her mother read. From June to September. From the end of school until its beginning. Year after year until her mother died.

Her father came for a week the end of August when summer sessions ended at the University. They drove to the station in her grandmother's old Chevrolet to meet him. Then he and Spencer fished. She went with him early mornings when the woods were still wet with night dew to pick blueberries for pancakes.

Anne sat back on her heels, holding the book against her chest, remembering.

There was the carnival. The last week in August, arriving almost simultaneously with her father, the carnival set up in a field at the edge of town, announcing itself with searchlights. It seemed to Anne that she waited all summer for her father and the carnival.

She remembered wandering up and down the rows of booths, holding his hand, knowing that beyond the spangled brightness of the carnival it was dark and late, past bedtime. She remembered the merry-go-round.

The two of them had a ride every summer. She remembered choosing the horse, the moment of anticipation before the ride began, the whirring of the motor, and then the music. The platform would begin to spin, their horse begin to rise and to sink, faster and faster until she imagined that it galloped. She held tight to the pole and screamed with pleasure, feeling the breeze lift her braids like ribbons. Whirling, galloping, dizzied with light, she wished that the ride would go on forever. She imagined the horse breaking loose from its pole. She imagined them galloping off into darkness. But almost before they'd begun, it seemed, she would feel the horse begin to slow, the music falter. Slowly the whirling stopped. Her braids fell back against her shoulders. Her father lifted her down.

She remembered wobbling off the platform, pulling his hand, looking up with dazzled eyes. "Again? Just once more?"

But there were never two rides. Only one each summer. Her mother stood in the shadow of the carousel, holding Anne's sweater, saying that it was time to go home.

Anne stared at the shelf of books before her. She remembered once she had shouted, *"No!"* The dazzle and the spin were still with her. She still held tight to her father's hand. "It's time to go home," her mother said firmly, and Anne looked up at her face and shouted, "No!"

Then, suddenly, her voice had died in her throat, and she threw herself against her mother's skirt, sobbing with fear.

Anne sat down on the rug. The book was clutched tight against her chest. As if it had happened a minute ago, she thought, and tried to laugh at herself. But the laugh didn't come, and when she replaced the book in the empty space on the shelf, her hands shook.

Mr. Babbitt rapped on the piano for attention, and the talking and laughing slowly died down. Music rattled. The pianist muddled through the opening chords of the accompaniment. "Muddled" was the right word, Anne thought irritably, and wondered why she hadn't noticed how badly the woman played before.

"Who is she?" she asked Laura as they started home.

"Mrs. Eaton. From school."

A little snow was falling again, dusting the dirty accumulation in the street. Laura whirled around, catching snow on her tongue. Anne watched her spinning on the sidewalk, looking at the wavering track she left in the snow, and thought of her mother playing the same carol many times better than Mrs. Eaton could ever hope to play it.

"She really mangles the accompaniment," she said.

"Well, she's mainly a gym teacher."

"Why don't they hire a pianist?"

Laura shrugged. "Who cares?" And she spun again, flapping her arms in the falling snow.

"*I* care," Anne said flatly. And then, "Are you going to keep doing that or can we walk home?"

Laura stopped whirling and fell into step beside her. "She's not *that* bad," Laura said. "She misses a few notes, but she tries."

"Actually she's rotten. She misses *half* the notes if you'd bother to notice."

Laura examined a snowflake on her mitten. "Well, I like her."

"That's because you don't know anything about music."

Laura glanced up. "No," she said quietly, "it's because I like her."

"You like her because you like her? Very good, Laura."

Laura looked at her with an expression that was half-hurt, half-puzzled. "What's the matter with *you*?" she said.

And at once Anne was sorry. She didn't know what the matter was. She had been wondering all afternoon. It wasn't Laura. It wasn't even the pianist, bad as she was. It was something heavy in her chest, something thick and stupid in her head. "I'm sorry," she said to Laura. "I shouldn't have said that."

"Why did you, then?"

"I don't know." And then, because it seemed to her that she was offering some sort of explanation, she said, "I'm trying to write this paper."

"So what?"

"I can't even get started. I can't seem to think any more."

"You?" Laura's voice was heavy with disbelief. "Maybe you're just tired."

Anne shook her head. "It isn't just the paper. I got a D on a midterm a few weeks ago."

Now Laura was truly stunned. "Your teacher must be a sadist."

"She's not. The D was generous, in fact." And it had been. Mrs. Liggett had done the best she could. She'd written a note on the returned exam inviting Anne to come in and discuss it, but Anne hadn't gone. There was nothing to discuss.

"I don't know why you worry so much about stuff like that," Laura said. "Look at me."

Anne looked at her going off down the street in her own direction, her coat drooping unevenly over the tops of her boots. For the first time in her life Anne envied her. It would be so simple to trudge through every day as Laura did, disheveled, unconcerned, minding things sometimes but not minding them much. Anne watched her disappearing in the snow-feathered twilight and knew that she herself would never be that way. She turned and started home, feeling exhausted.

She was barely aware that she was home until, stupidly, she registered lights ahead and the dispirited little car crouching in the open garage.

In the upstairs hall she encountered Dory, stocking-footed, holding an armload of sheets. "Come see what I've done," Dory said. "I finally got around to putting in new shelf paper."

Anne looked into the linen closet.

"It looks pretty good, don't you think?" Dory said.

Anne nodded. "Except that the towels go on the top shelf."

A little later Dory knocked at her door. Anne looked up from the bed where she was sitting. "Can we talk?" Dory said.

"Sure."

Dory padded across the room and sat down on the foot of the bed. "You know, Anne, I'll never be able to do things the way your mother did."

Anne looked at the rug between her knees and said nothing. Not Dory, not the pianist. Nobody could do things the way her mother did.

"I know it makes things different for you," Dory said. "Maybe not much like home."

She moved her hand toward Anne as if to touch her, hesitated. "But it *is* your home. You were here first. I worry sometimes that you're feeling uncomfortable because of me."

Anne looked down at the hand resting on the bedspread between them. She imagined touching it. She thought of Dory bending to help her sweep up the scraps of broken plate. She shook her head.

"It's not because of you," she said slowly, knowing that the words were true. It wasn't Dory. The feeling that was troubling her hadn't much to do with Dory at all.

Thirteen

On Friday afternoon in a light snowfall Anne set out to finish her Christmas shopping. The streets that bordered the campus were lined with shops. Behind their plate-glass windows were Shetland sweaters in rainbow stacks, hiking boots with corrugated soles, pyramids of books, records propped against tape recorders. Nothing she saw attracted her.

She walked past the windows slowly, hoping that one of them would contain an inspiration. But amid the bits of holly and tinsel decorating the displays were objects intended for college students or professors. There was nothing that seemed right for Dory.

She passed a window filled with a variety of pipes,

another with Japanese calligraphy tools. She crossed the street. At the corner a man in a red vest was ringing a bell. People stopped to put change in the bucket he held. Money for the hospital. Anne dropped a quarter into the bucket. He gave her a tag to wear, and she looped it over a coat button, walking on.

More sweaters. More books. A pizza shop, its window laced with frost. Anne stopped for a minute to watch a man kneading dough, turned to go on, and saw Eric. He was coming toward her carrying packages, and he had very nearly reached her before she saw him. He smiled, stopped smiling, then smiled again as if in a second he had made a series of calculations about how he felt, how to behave.

"Are you shopping?"

She nodded.

"So am I." He nodded at his parcels. "I just bought Sam a Swiss army knife."

And he had given money to the hospital. There was a red tag attached to the zipper of his jacket.

"He'll like that," Anne said.

"I think so."

In the window behind him the man flipped dough into the air.

"I'm almost finished," Anne said. "I have only one more present to buy."

The dough flipped up and descended. Eric dug his hands into the pockets of his jacket, pressing his packages against his side. "That's not much," he said. "That shouldn't take long."

"No."

They hesitated on the sidewalk, two fixed points in a moving stream of shoppers. Anne could think of nothing more to say. She stood silent, looking at the snowflakes that settled and melted on his jacket and on his hair—like confetti, she thought, on his dark hair. And all at once she wanted to touch him, to put out her hand and feel the slippery fabric of his jacket under her mitten. He said something that she didn't hear. She was remembering her hand in the curve of his palm, walking home slowly, last summer, in the dark.

"I guess I'd better get on with it," he said. She nodded, unable to speak. Her hands were fists in the pockets of her coat.

He hesitated, waiting for something. Waiting for her to say something, she thought. And then he turned.

She watched him walk away, dodging shoppers. She watched his jacket weaving through the crowd until he disappeared. She had not moved.

On the other side of the window the man flipped dough. He caught it and winked at her. Anne didn't smile. She put her hand against the plate-glass window, felt the cold through her mitten, and turned away.

The church seemed chillier than usual. The carols barely held her attention. It was their last rehearsal, and it ran late again as Mr. Babbitt struggled with one of the soprano parts.

"Be here half an hour early on Monday," he said as they were gathering their coats. Monday was Christmas Eve.

When they came out of church they saw Mrs. Dewitt

parked across the street. "Will you look at that?" said Laura. "A miracle has occurred."

The car—a dented Ford station wagon—was wheezing clouds of exhaust into the twilight. Mrs. Dewitt leaned out the window and called to them. "In case I might not recognize her, I suppose," Laura said. "In case there might be two cars like that in town."

They waited for a car to pass and crossed the street. Laura jerked open the back door. "What's the occasion?" she said. "Is it a family emergency, or did you finish your dissertation?"

"It's one of the puppies." Mrs. Dewitt pushed back her straggling bang of hair. "I want you to ride over to the vet's with me."

Anne followed Laura into the car, and they leaned over the front seat to see what Mrs. Dewitt was talking about. The puppy lay nestled in a shoebox on the seat, carefully wrapped in a piece of terry cloth towel.

"What's wrong with him?" Laura said.

"I can't tell for sure. But he's terribly lethargic and he's breathing strangely. I could tell that Gwendolyn was worried."

Anne could see that Mrs. Dewitt was worried. She stabbed out her cigarette in the ashtray and put the car into gear. "Why can't I get the heater to come on, Laura?"

"Mainly," Laura said dryly, "because it's been broken for about two years."

"And we never got it fixed?"

"Of course we never got it fixed. Slow down."

Mrs. Dewitt put on the brake and looked apologetically into the rear-view mirror. She was still wearing her fuzzy old writing slippers. She hadn't taken time even to put on boots, Anne thought.

"How come you waited for us if you were worried?" Laura said. "Why didn't you take him right away?"

Mrs. Dewitt half-turned to look at them. "I just didn't want to go alone," she said, and Laura seemed to understand this. She leaned over her mother's shoulder. "It probably isn't anything serious," she said. "I'll bet it's just a cold."

Mrs. Dewitt shook her head and lit another cigarette, fumbling with the lighter, eyes on the street. "I don't think puppies that small *get* colds," she said. "Don't they have natural immunity or something?"

The car was growing cloudy with smoke, but Laura, who would ordinarily have complained, said nothing. "It *could* be a cold," was all she said.

Anne leaned over and looked at the puppy again. It was lying unnaturally still in the shoebox. She thought of it struggling to stand on the slippery kitchen floor, struggling and failing, again and again. She reached down and touched its side gently. Its ribs rose and fell unevenly under her fingertips.

Mrs. Dewitt paused at a corner, waiting to turn left. She drummed her fingernails on the steering wheel impatiently. Anne stared at the lights of the oncoming cars.

In another block Mrs. Dewitt slowed and pulled into a parking lot. Across the street the windows of the veterinary clinic were soft blots of light in the dusk. Mrs. Dewitt maneuvered into an empty space and turned off the engine. "You come with me, will you, Laura?"

Anne watched them, carrying the shoebox between them, cross the street and go up the steps into the building. The wreath on the door swung back and forth slowly after the door closed. It seemed only a few minutes —too short a time—before it opened again and she saw the two of them coming out. They walked arm in arm across the parking lot to the car.

Laura pulled open the door. "He was already dead," she said simply.

"But he was breathing five minutes ago. I touched him."

"I guess he died after that."

Anne leaned into the front seat and looked at the place where, minutes before, the shoebox had been. "Maybe I shouldn't have touched him," she said.

"No," Laura said. "He just died, that's all."

Mrs. Dewitt got into the car and began to search in her purse for the keys. "I shouldn't have waited for you," she said. "I should have brought him right away the minute I noticed."

"It probably wouldn't have made a difference," Laura said.

"I don't know. Maybe he was that way all day and I didn't notice. I was up in the attic, and I just didn't notice."

Laura leaned over the front seat and put her arms

around her mother's neck. "You couldn't help it, Mama," she said softly. "It wasn't your fault."

Anne watched them, transfixed. She was filled with a longing so sharp that she closed her eyes. Then Laura sat back and Anne heard the engine start.

They drove in silence going home, passing the same corners, the same stoplights that they had passed before, but driving slowly now. Laura sniffed and blew her nose. Anne looked out the window. Always looking through windows, she thought, and pressed her mittened hand against the glass as if to reach through.

In front of the house Mrs. Dewitt stopped to let Anne out. Laura climbed into the front seat. "I'm sorry about the puppy," Anne said, and closed the door.

She stood on the curb watching until the Dewitts' taillights disappeared around the corner, and then she turned toward the house. She had forgotten that Dory and her father were going out, although as soon as she saw the empty garage she remembered Dory's telling her. Spencer, too, would be out, celebrating the end of finals. And so she was alone.

There was cold chicken for supper, Dory had said, but Anne wasn't hungry. She wandered into the living room and sat down on the sofa that was littered with Spencer's books—political science, calculus, French. She didn't bother to move them.

The house creaked with its ghost sounds. Against her back were the crewel cushions her mother had made. If she ran her fingers along the base of the lamp, she would feel the glued seam of a repair made long ago. She knew the house by heart, by touch, but in all these old remembered things there was no comfort.

She thought of the puppy, alive and then dead, already gathered away into memory. She thought of Laura and her mother, the quick sympathy between them and the easy embrace. She thought of Eric.

Suddenly she could no longer bear the silence of the house. She stood up and walked to the piano, played some chords simply to fill the room with sound. She imagined the notes pushing their way through the tissue of remembered sounds that seemed to weigh so heavily in the room. And then, curious to know if it was still there, she lifted the seat of the piano bench and saw her old red music book.

The margins of the music were filled with directions written in her mother's hand. "Slow a little here." "Softly!" Anne flipped the pages until she came to "Humoresque." Here the comments stopped midway through the score, stopped at exactly the spot where she had stopped in learning the piece.

Anne frowned at the notes and began to play. The silly melody that she had once considered beautiful bounced under her fingers as foolishly as Dory's song, as mindlessly as needles clicking their way through yarn. She could almost hear her mother's voice counting the rhythm, her cadence as steady as a metronome. Anne squinted at the music and felt her fingers stiffen. She remembered that they had always stiffened midway in this music so that then, as now, she could no longer play. *Count, Anne.* But it was no good counting when her fingers had frozen, stubborn as sticks, on the keys. Carefully she lifted her hands, as though the smooth yellow ivory had grown treacherous as ice.

In the kitchen she ate the chicken Dory had left and washed her plate. When she finished, it was still early. She turned on the television in the study, watched for a half hour and was bored. Finally she went upstairs to her room. The loneliness that she had felt all evening pursued her. The bedroom was cold. She took her nightgown and robe out of the closet, pulled off her sweater and started automatically to put it away.

Tissue paper rustled as she pulled open the drawer. The neatly wrapped package slid toward her. Slowly Anne lifted it from the drawer, folded back the tissue and looked at the sweater. She remembered its wide, ribbed yoke, remembered her mother wrapping it and tucking it into her school trunk. She sat back on her heels with the sweater in her lap, and suddenly, as though a film had begun to unreel, a parade of clothes came marching out of memory. Blue. Everything blue. Blue and more blue all her life, because, she had been told, it was a color that was pretty with their hair, hers and her mother's. She looked away. With a certainty that left her motionless, half-bent above the drawer, she knew that she hated that color. Hated it now and always had.

Quickly she wadded up the tissue paper. She dropped the sweater into the drawer and closed it. The sweater she had taken off lay folded on the floor. She left it there, unwilling to open the drawer again.

Later, in bed, she heard the car in the driveway and footsteps coming upstairs. Much later she heard Spencer. She could tell by the noises he made on the stairs that he had had a lot of beer. "Spencer," she called softly.

He pushed open the door and she saw him silhouetted in the light from the hall. "You still awake?"

"Are you drunk?"

"Celebrational," he said. "Filled with joy." He came into the room and sat down on the end of her bed. "What's up?"

"Spencer, something happened, didn't it, a long time ago?"

"Hannibal crossed the Alps."

"To us, I mean."

"To you and me?"

"I think so."

Spencer yawned and leaned back on his elbows. "A lot of things have happened to us, Annsie. Too many to recount in the middle of the night."

"Spencer, did we ever go away someplace at Christmastime? Just us?"

There was a long pause, so long that she thought he had fallen asleep. Finally he said, "You know we did."

"I don't remember."

"Well," he said, "we did. Once."

Anne sat up, shivering, and pulled the bedclothes around her. "Tell me."

Spencer shook his head, a movement she could just see in the light from the hall. "Look," he said, "it's late. It's nearly morning. If you want to talk tomorrow, fine. But not tonight. Okay, pal?"

She didn't insist. She lay down and listened to the sounds Spencer made getting ready for bed. She listened to a car pass and watched its lights slide slowly across the ceiling. Then it was quiet, and she listened to the silence of the house.

Fourteen

Anne woke at five and couldn't sleep again. She watched the glowing hands of the clock move to five-thirty, then six. She had awakened with music spinning through her mind, clickity-clacking mindlessly like the wheels of a train. She folded the pillow under her head and stared into the darkness.

At six-thirty the room began, almost imperceptibly, to grow light. Not light really, Anne thought—but a paler shade of darkness. She stared at the hands of the clock another quarter of an hour and gave up trying to sleep.

Standing at her window, she watched the sky begin to turn a pale, liquid gray, and, abruptly, she decided to go skating.

The sprinklers had run all night, and the pond's surface was perfectly smooth. She skated once across it diagonally, leaving the first white cut in the ice. The rising sun, still hidden behind the bare trees, was staining their frozen branches pink.

She skated slowly around the periphery of the pond. The air was perfectly still. The sound of a car door slamming seemed to hang suspended in the stillness. Anne glided around the gradual curve of ice.

It seemed effortless even as she began to skate faster. The rhythm was quite different from the rhythm of running—fluid and swooping, like the flight of a swallow. She felt strong and easy with it, swooping as if she were carried on wings.

Ahead of her the ice was turning rosy, reflecting the sunrise. She skated into the color and through it, winging her way across the stretch of rose-colored ice. Then back onto ice that was still blue-violet, at the end of the pond that the sun hadn't reached.

She listened to the whispering sound her skates made. She exhaled and watched her breath turn pink and cloudy in the frozen air. She couldn't remember when it had felt so good to skate.

The sun crept slowly up behind the trees, seeming not to move but steadily moving, so that each time Anne circled the pond it was a little higher in relation to the branches. And then it appeared above them and dazzled her with light.

Throwing out her arms and pulling them in, Anne went

into a spin. She hadn't remembered she knew how to spin, but her skates found their way into the figure. Around and around she went, using her arms to keep the momentum. Her body remembered the movement. Her skates drew together, one behind the other; her arms pulled her smoothly into the turn.

She whirled. Her head snapped around, seeing trees, seeing sun, a yellow brick house, the elementary school chimney—trees, sun, house, school. Flying around in a brilliant circle of glittering sun and colored ice.

When she began to slow, she pushed off again, spinning through rose and blue and violet and sunshine bright as carnival lights. The wind of the spinning made music in her ears, light and gay—a carousel tune. Rising and falling, tingling with pleasure. Trees, sun, house, school, rose, glitter, violet, blue. Spinning wind. A carousel tune. Complicated music with sharps and flats. *What is the key of four sharps, Anne?*

The circle of key signs. The circling whirl. The old red book. The merry-go-round. *Anne, are you counting? Are you counting, Anne?*

And suddenly the spinning stopped. Anne was pitching forward into air. In that moment she knew she had caught an edge. The blue ice came up to meet her face.

Chords crashed. Clotted notes sharp as splintered ice reverberated in her head. The crashing of piano keys. A sound that rocked off the living room walls, bouncing off stiff shards of sunlight, tearing a gash across the rug.

For a moment furious white light and then darkness.

Dropping down and down on a current of darkness. Darkness folding gently around her like wings.

Gradually she knew that her cheek was numb. That it rested on ice. That the sharp staccato sounds she heard were her own breathing and that she lay sprawled, sucking air. She had fallen.

She remembered the ice rising toward her, and the impact. Shaking, she raised herself on one arm. She knew that she remembered other things.

She sat up slowly. Her ankle hurt. She looked at it lying before her on the ice like something that was not her own. Carefully she loosened the skate and eased the tongue back until she could see the sock underneath. Her foot moved. Her ankle was not broken, then. Possibly sprained.

Bracing with her arms, she shoved herself up onto her good leg. Moving gingerly, she pushed along on one skate to the edge of the pond and hobbled to a bench on the warming shack porch.

For several minutes she sat staring blankly at her foot, but it was not her foot she saw. With a clarity that astonished her, she saw something else—a child sitting upright in a train.

Anne closed her eyes. She knew the train's destination. It was going to Wisconsin. It was roaring toward a lake in Wisconsin through a Christmas snowstorm. Over the river and through the woods.

The child was sitting straight, having turned from the window, sternly holding a blue plush rabbit in her lap.

Across the aisle was a woman in a purple hat reading Ross Macdonald. The lights of the station had disappeared. There was nothing to see beyond the window but darkness and the reflected lights of the bright, hot car on the glass.

"Why are we going?" She had asked before and been told, but now she asked again, turning to the thin, serious boy in the seat beside her.

"You know."

"But tell me."

"Why do I have to tell you again? Everyone's told you."

Why? Because she needed to hear it again and again in case, just once, she might hear something else. "Once more. Please."

He sighed and put down the crossword puzzle he'd been working on. "We are going to Grandma's because Mother has gone away to live by herself."

Each time she asked, she held her breath, believing, each time, that the answer might have changed. She was only eight.

After a while there was the second question. "Why can't we stay home with Daddy?" Again, she knew, but she needed to keep asking. They had stayed with their father alone since before Thanksgiving. In the evening, when he came home, he read her stories while she sat beside him in his chair. When she sat there she forgot the afternoons that seemed so strange in the house without her mother, with only Ellen ironing in the kitchen. "Why can't we?" she said.

"Because he can't manage."

What did it mean—manage? And why couldn't he? It was nice hearing stories in her father's chair. He didn't remember when it was time for bed. He didn't remember to ask if she'd practiced.

"Over vacation he's going to try to work things out."

"What things?" Although she'd been told.

"Work things out with Mother. You know."

He turned back to his puzzle. She looked at her reflection in the glass. After a while she said, "Why does she want to live by herself?"

He was exasperated. He looked at her, and his glasses, like the train window, reflected light. "Because she needs some space to think."

This was the oddest answer of all. Anne could understand space to move in, but she didn't know about space to think. She didn't believe this could be the right answer. She held her rabbit. One eye was loose and she pressed it hard against the cloth, trying to make it stick.

Then there was a new question, one she hadn't asked before, although she thought of it every day.

"Spencer," she said. "When she left, was it because of me?"

He sighed. "Of course not."

But a deep, sick feeling that it might be so had been gathering for a long time at the corners of her mind, and in spite of what he said, it stayed with her. She had slammed her hands on the piano keys. She had screamed at her mother. She had refused to work any longer on the piece she couldn't learn. And in that terrible moment while sounds tore the room with blinding white dissonance, she had wished that her mother would disappear.

She thought about it at night in bed at her grandmother's, staring at the ceiling, but she didn't cry. She was afraid to cry. It seemed to her that all her feelings were tangled inside her and that, if she cried, she might then scream and smash things. And so she stared at the ceiling at night or watched moonlight puddle on the bedroom floor and wondered why people went away. If they loved you, did they go? Or was it that if you screamed they stopped loving?

Anne stared at the sock, the swelling ankle. The throbbing in her ankle seemed only an extension of the pain that engulfed her as she forced herself to remember the child. At her grandmother's there was a large box on Christmas morning and in it a pair of new white skates. She had never had such a pair of skates. They were a message from her mother.

Each day she carried her skates to the lake. Each day she practiced taking small, uncertain steps on the precarious blades. Often she fell. Often she lay discouraged on the ice, staring at its speckled surface and at the leaves of the pin oaks frozen under the surface, but she never cried.

She pushed herself up and started again, practicing short steps. Every day. Because she told herself that when she learned to skate well enough, her mother would come home. Everything depended on that.

And it worked. Although she had only begun to learn to glide, Spencer told her one day that they were going home. He said their mother had returned.

Both her mother and father were at the station to meet the train. She saw them through the window as the train slowed down. She didn't smile or wave. She stood looking at them from behind the protection of the glass, and they seemed to her peculiarly small—like figures seen through a telescope turned around.

When they wanted to kiss her, she stood still and let them. When, later, they wanted to talk about it, she wouldn't talk.

Her mother sat beside her on her bed at night and tried to explain. Anne remembered her thin hand lying between them on the folded edge of the sheet. But Anne had turned away, afraid to touch it. She had put her face into the pillow, already beginning to forget.

Fifteen

Pain flickered along her shin. Anne realized that she was very cold. She needed to move.

She touched her ankle carefully. When she pressed it, pain darted down along her foot and up the shinbone. She wondered whether, if she moved slowly, she could walk on it. Then, looking around the empty expanse of park, she knew that she would have to try.

She took off her skates and, gritting her teeth, eased the swollen ankle into a boot. Hopping, pausing to catch her breath, hopping again, Anne made her way slowly along the edge of the park, balancing with the toe of her aching foot.

She had no sense of how long it took to cover the few blocks between the park and the house. It didn't occur to her to stop anyplace along the way to ask for help. Her legs were sturdy from running. She felt strong and quiet, moved by the simple necessity to reach home.

Dory met her at the door. "I saw you coming. You've hurt yourself."

"I hurt my ankle."

"Thank heavens your father left the car home this morning." Then Dory reached out her arms and Anne collapsed against her.

The young doctor in the emergency room held the X-ray up to the light. "No break," he said cheerfully. "Just a sprain. I'll wrap it in an elastic bandage and give you something for pain."

Anne looked at the bones of her ankle, gray specters floating on the black film.

"You'll have to stay off it for a few days," the doctor said.

"I have to sing in a choir Christmas Eve," she replied.

"You'll have to see how it feels by then."

"But I've promised to sing."

The doctor glanced up. "Look," he said, "take it easy. There are some things you have no control over."

The words reached into the quietness that was growing within her, and Anne nodded, looked at the bandage he was winding neatly around her foot, looked at the fuzzy ghost bones on the X-ray film, and sighed.

He helped her into the hall, where Dory was waiting, and handed Dory a prescription for pills. "Keep her off the foot," he said. "It needs time to heal."

Dory stood up. Gratefully, Anne leaned her weight on

Dory's small shoulder, and together, slowly, they made their way down the hall.

At home Dory propped Anne on the sofa in the study. "So you won't have to be alone upstairs," she said. She wrapped a blanket around her and tucked it loosely around her feet.

"Don't you have to go to work?" Anne said.

"For a little while. I'll drop in there and then come back with your prescription."

Anne listened to the car choking as Dory backed out. She was terribly sleepy. The room drifted around her. It seemed delicious to be lying doing nothing because there was nothing she could do. She felt herself sinking and floating, falling asleep and knowing, luxuriously, that she was falling. There are some things you can't control. She sank, letting herself sink—finally, gratefully, letting herself go.

When she woke, Dory was sitting in the wing chair, knitting. "How does it feel?" she said.

Anne moved her ankle under the blanket. "It hurts."

"What about one of the pain pills? You can have one every four hours, the bottle says."

Anne turned her head back and forth on the pillow. "I want to feel it," she said.

"What on earth for, honey?"

Anne didn't try to explain. She closed her eyes. It was simply that she wanted to feel it—her ankle and all the rest. She wanted to lie there and feel it, letting it heal, aware of the pain until it went away.

Anne dozed and woke all afternoon. Whenever she woke, Dory was still there in the wing chair, knitting. Whenever she woke, she felt the ache in her ankle and the ache of the memory as if they were one—quiet, steady aches that would heal if she let them.

She looked at the bookshelves with drowsy eyes. There are things you can't control, the doctor had said. Can't control and don't make happen. It wasn't because of her that her mother had died.

Anne tucked an arm under her head. Had she ever really thought so? And then, yes, she knew that she had.

It was the sweater lying in her trunk on the first day of school. Her roommate chatted while they unpacked, and Anne tried to listen, but, looking at the tissue paper package, she lost track.

Shades of rose and blue and violet streamed through her memory and, with them, the steady sound of needles clicking, the steady cadence of the voice, the words that had gone on and on, insisting, falling endlessly as rain. Staring at the package, her head swam.

"I don't want to go there. I don't *want* to go!" She remembered saying it more than once. It hadn't mattered. It never had. She had been swept once more on the current of her mother's words until, like a twig, she had come to rest here at this school where she had never wanted to be. Her roommate clattered wire hangers. Anne looked at the package at the top of the trunk.

She couldn't touch it. She had lifted out the clothes beneath and left it lying in the trunk. It had lain there a year, untouched, before she brought it home and hid it in the back of the bureau drawer.

Anne shifted on the sofa. Six weeks after that first day at school, her mother was dead. Six weeks and hundreds of miles away from that day. And yet, in the moments following her father's phone call, Anne thought first of the sweater, frightened as a small girl giddy from the carousel, guilty as the child riding the train. Half a dozen times she slept and woke, drifted in and out of sleep like an exhausted traveler. She was still dozing when her father came home. He was standing beside the sofa before she was fully awake.

"How are you feeling?" He looked down at her.

"I'm all right. My ankle hurts, that's all."

"What happened, Annsie, do you know?"

"I think I caught an edge."

Someone had lighted a fire that crackled, making patterns on the wall. Her father pulled up a chair and sat down beside her. "Wasn't that pretty early to go skating alone? I don't suppose there was anyone around to help at that time of day."

"No. But I managed."

Frowning, her father began to fill his pipe. "I don't think it was a very good idea," he said.

"Well, I can't do it again for a while anyway." No skating. No running. Nothing to do but lie there and think.

He tapped the tobacco thoughtfully. "Your mother used to go skating that way."

Anne remembered. She had watched her mother set out for the pond, walking quickly, skates over her shoulder on gray November mornings. "That was the year she left us, wasn't it?" Anne said quietly. "That was the year she skated early in the morning."

Her father nodded. "Mainly that year."

"Why did she leave us?" Anne realized it was the same question she had repeated over and over the year she was eight.

He tapped his pipe. "Oh, Annie, why do people do things? You're old enough to know that sometimes people don't know themselves. She thought she was unhappy. She needed to think."

There was a pause while he lighted his pipe. Anne watched the match flame lighting the deep, tired crevices in his face, and the question reshaped itself, becoming the question that she had not been able to put into words at eight: If she loved me, why did she leave me? Anne took a deep breath.

That was one of the questions, but it was only one. Beneath it there was another. It had been swimming at the edges of her mind for days, darting away as a fish does, startled by a movement that comes too close. She thought she could not avoid it any more, and so she pushed herself down one more time, like a diver. She knew the question had always been there, unspeakable, at the bottom of all she remembered and had chosen to forget. And she made herself ask: Did I ever love my mother at all?

She held it, an object fished from deep water. And,

while her father fussed with his pipe, she began to try to answer it.

In the long afternoon's dozing she remembered many things. The years of trying to please her mother, of trying not to be angry and to be in control. But there were other memories, as real as the anger.

Once, during the sleepy afternoon she had awakened, remembering the time she had had pneumonia. Her mother had sat night after night, all night, beside her bed, in case she should wake and be worse. The fever had made her head ache. Her mother had sometimes rocked her. Sitting in her mother's lap, rocking and drowsy, leaning against her, Anne had not known where her own body stopped and her mother's began.

Was that love? Anne didn't know. It was the oldest, deepest feeling she knew, and so she called it love. Not easy love. Neither of them was ever easy. But love all the same. Love as old and hard as chipped flint.

Blue smoke quivered up from her father's pipe. She reached for his hand. He held her palm as if he were going to read her fortune. "You never wanted to talk about the time your mother left," he said. "We always could have. We still could."

Anne shook her head. "Sometime we will. Not now."

There were questions that she might ask sometime, but they were for later. For now she understood enough. She had found the hardest question. She had answered it. They had loved each other in their imperfect ways. And it was all right. Anne breathed gently. All right.

Laura arrived in the morning with a chocolate chip cookie, six inches wide, wrapped in foil. "I made it," she said. "It was all I could think of. I mean, what do you give somebody with a sprained ankle?"

Anne broke the cookie into pieces and offered Laura half. "I can't sing tomorrow night," she said. "I won't be able to stand that long."

"I know. I told Babbitt you probably couldn't. You know what he said? That he figured nobody'd hear the altos in that case. The sadist."

"How did you know I might not be able to?"

"Oh. Well, she—" Laura floundered for words. "I don't know what to call her. Your father's wife, you know. She called."

"Dory. She probably wouldn't mind if you called her that. Or you could call her Mrs. Cameron."

"That's what I called your mother."

"Well, it's Dory's name now," Anne said. "So you might as well call her that."

There was confusion in the house all afternoon. Dory made Christmas cookies, which she burned. Spencer and their father struggled to set up the tree. Anne hobbled into the living room to watch them. When she was tired, she hobbled back to lie down.

She thought a great deal between dozes. About her mother. About the two of them. About Dory and her father and about Eric. Sometime late in the afternoon she thought about her Conrad paper. That was something that she could work on lying down. The paper seemed less difficult to write now. She had a week left to finish it. She thought that she could. This settled, she slept and, after enough sleeping, she woke, and that day slid into the next, and it was Christmas Eve.

They decorated the tree, which stood like an ungainly giant in the living room. Anne, foot propped, handed ornaments to Spencer. Later their father made his Christmas punch.

Anne limped into the kitchen to watch him. Dory, on tiptoe, was peering into the pot. The steaming wine made ringlets of the wispy hair around her face. Behind her, like the White Knight in *Alice*, stood Anne's father, adding spices to his invented brew.

"It smells wonderful!" Dory said, looking up at him with a steam-damp, shining face. Watching them, Anne felt her throat grow tight.

Suddenly she knew what she would give Dory. Limping, she climbed the stairs to her room, found paper and ribbon, and wrapped a small package.

And then it was Christmas. There was a sweater for her from Dory that was exactly the wrong shade—a Kool-Aid green. But Anne could picture Dory buying it—standing in the store in her boots with the run-over heels, intent on getting it right. And so she put it on and wore it Christmas Day.

Dory unwrapped Anne's present the way she had unwrapped everything else—like a child overcome with the immensity of the day. "Oh," she said. "Oh, Anne, where did this come from?"

"Mrs. Mortimer gave it to me," Anne said. "I thought you might like to have it."

"You look about twenty in this picture," Dory said to Anne's father.

"Nope. Thirty-four," he said. "I was thirty-four years old when I built that crazy feeder. Remember, Anne? I built it the year you were eight."

"Nine."

He had built it after the bad time was over. She remembered discovering it in the yard between the houses when they returned from the lake in September, just after her birthday. At first she thought he'd built it for her.

She was wrong. "I built it for your mother," he said. "I built it for a welcome home."

Anne was not disappointed. She was glad that he had built it for her mother. She was glad when it made her mother laugh.

Sixteen

On the last day, Anne packed the few clothes she had brought with her. She tucked her notebook with the half-finished Conrad paper into the side pocket of the bag where she could reach it easily if, on the plane, she decided to write. Spencer had said they should leave at noon. They were all going.

After breakfast, while the others were drinking coffee, she left the table and went upstairs. It took time, even after a week, to climb the steps. It took even longer to make her way up the steep flight to the attic. She was out of breath when she reached the top.

She stood in the darkness for a minute before she turned on the light, smelling the old scent of dust and cedar. Then she switched on the bulb and limped across the attic floor to the bag that contained her mother's clothes.

Soft fabrics and soft colors and the fading smell of mothballs. She touched the shoulder of her mother's velvet evening coat.

She remembered the coat. She remembered the two of them setting off in the evening, so splendid in their evening clothes that they seemed like strangers. And she remembered waking much later and feeling her mother beside her, stroking her hair.

She stroked the coat now—the splendid coat that nobody would ever wear again—and knew deeply, and for the first time without fear, that her mother was dead.

She put her face against the soft velvet as if it were a shoulder. And then she wept, weeping for her mother, telling her good-bye.

Spencer found her standing there when he came up the stairs—looking for her, she supposed. For once he didn't say a word. He put his arm around her shoulders and stood silently beside her. She knew his face would be quiet and grave, as she had seen it years ago on the train. They stood together there for a long time, and then Spencer said they'd better get ready to leave.

The plane rolled down the runway and stopped, waiting for its turn to take off. Anne looked back at the terminal behind them, misty in light-falling snow. Spencer and Dory and her father would be walking back to the parking lot. Laura would be at school. She thought she would write to Eric in a day or so and try to explain to him some part of what had happened. It wouldn't be simple to do. He might not care. But she would try.

The engines roared louder. The plane began to roll forward, gathering speed. Anne sat back in her seat and felt the power of the engines as the plane raced down the runway, pushing at the wind. Then she heard the wheels leave the ground and, eyes closed, she felt the climb begin.